SHADOWLAND

SHADOWLAND

The Brotherhood of the Conch: Book III

A NOVEL BY

CHITRA LEKHA BANERJEE DIVAKARUNI

A Neal Porter Book
ROARING BROOK PRESS
New York

A Neal Porter Book
Published by Roaring Brook Press
Roaring Brook Press is a division of Holtzbrinck Publishing Holdings Limited Partnership
175 Fifth Avenue, New York, New York 10010
www.roaringbrookpress.com

Distributed in Canada by H. B. Fenn and Company, Ltd.

Cataloging-in-Publication Data is on file at the Library of Congress.
ISBN-13: 978-1-59643-153-9
ISBN-10: 1-59643-153-9

Roaring Brook Press books are available for special promotions and premiums.
For details contact: Director of Special Markets, Holtzbrinck Publishers.

Book design by Jennifer Browne
First edition April 2009
Printed in February 2009 in the United States of America by
RR Donnelley, Harrisonburg, Virginia
2 4 6 8 10 9 7 5 3 1

For my three men,
Murthy, Abhay, and Anand,
who believed in me
from the very first.

And for Juno,
who sat beside me every day,
while I wrote this book.

DISASTER!

Anand paced up and down the length of the cave, which was dimly lit by a sputtering lamp that was threatening to extinguish itself. His footsteps echoed against the cave's damp, rough-hewn walls. He was vexed, and who could blame him? He'd been waiting here in this freezing hole high on a cliffside for four days now—the last twenty-four hours without food or water. And there was still no sight or sound of the hermit he'd come all this way to meet! If he hadn't seen the man himself on a couple of occasions in the past year, clambering up the side of a distant crag like a skinny goat, his gray hair blown helter-skelter and his robe billowing in the wind, he would have doubted his very existence in spite of all that Abhaydatta, the Master Healer, had told him.

Though Anand, as Abhaydatta's apprentice, held the healer in the greatest esteem, right now he was angry with him as well. If it weren't for Abhaydatta, Anand wouldn't be here, starving half to death, and probably coming down with a terrible cold, too. His head felt like it was stuffed with wool, and the sounds he heard were distorted and indistinct, as though reaching him from very far away. Anand was partially to blame for the situation in which he found himself, but when this unpleasant thought pricked at his conscience, he pushed it away.

I'll wait until the lamp burns out, he thought. *Then I'll go back down to the Silver Valley, where I'll have to tell Abhaydatta that I failed.*

He sat down on the clammy, uncomfortably sharp rocks just inside the entrance to the cave, crouching a little, for he'd grown a great deal in the last year since he turned fifteen and wasn't yet used to his height. From this vantage point he scanned the hillside for the hermit, though his hopes were not high. He drew his yellow wool tunic, the one that all apprentices wore, closer and pushed his long hair away from his eyes. The despondence that tormented him today was unusual for him. Generally he was cheerful and responsible, much liked by the healers. His fellow apprentices liked him, too, though they sometimes complained that he took the world too seriously. But mostly they held him in awe because he held a special position in the Brotherhood. He was keeper of the magical conch from which the healers drew their power, and the only one with whom the conch communicated. Anand, however, was rather modest and did not consider himself special. If anything, he had many doubts about his abilities—and all of them seemed to have surfaced today.

After four days of harsh winds and sleet, it was finally bright outside, the sun shining on piles of snow. It was still cold—but then, up this high in the Himalayas, it was always cold, except in the Silver Valley, where right now Anand's schoolmates would be sitting down to a hot, savory lunch. Gloom descended on him as he imagined their meal. On Tuesdays—today *was* Tuesday, wasn't it?—the cooks served a hearty rice-and-lentil stew filled with fresh vegetables grown in the valley, with fried potatoes on the side. His stomach growled as he imagined biting into a succulent, spicy potato. Then his appetite ebbed. How would Abhaydatta react to his failure—and to his disobedience, for he had given Anand strict instructions to return to the valley yesterday? Abhaydatta wasn't given to ranting. He would probably stride away, lips clamped together in disappointment. But some of the other apprentices were sure to make fun of Anand.

Anand did not know that none of the things he dreaded was going to happen, that something far worse was waiting for him in the valley.

ᝌ

Five days ago. That was when it had all started.

Anand had been in the middle of a lesson with Master Mihirdatta, the healer who specialized in Transformation, a skill that allowed a healer to examine the very essence of objects and change the whirling particles of energy that were at their core.

"If you can focus your intellect enough to get down to the level of this energy in something, if you can feel its particular vibration, then you can change it when necessary to something else," Mihirdatta explained. "But it is an advanced skill even for those of you who are senior apprentices, and not to be undertaken lightly, for to change the essence of even the smallest object is dangerous and may have far-reaching consequences, either on the universe or on the healer." He gave the students a simple exercise: to change the palm leaf on which they were writing their notes into parchment.

Anand concentrated the way the healer had explained, closing his eyes, drifting into a state that could best be described as alert sleep, and trying to feel deep into the fabric of the leaf. Just when he felt as though the leaf was dissolving into a pool of rapidly moving pinpricks of light, he was distracted by the arrival of a messenger. It was Raj-bhanu, a friend of Anand's. They had been on an adventure together when Raj-bhanu was a senior apprentice. He had recently graduated and had been given a junior healer's robes. He bowed to Mihirdatta in apology for the interruption. However, he said, he had an urgent message from Abhaydatta. Anand was to meet him in the Hall of Seeing as soon as he finished this class.

This was highly unusual. The apprentices' days followed a strict and—in Anand's opinion—overly predictable routine. The other boys whispered among themselves, throwing Anand curious glances. Anand sat up very straight, his heart beating fast as he wondered why his mentor had summoned him. He knew it was important. Otherwise Abhaydatta would not have interrupted his lessons. He hoped it was something exciting.

Anand loved being part of the Brotherhood and learning the secret arts with which they aided the world. He knew how lucky he was to live here, in this sheltered valley with its winding paths lined by silver-barked parijat trees, its airy dormitories, and its magnificent Crystal Hall where the conch was housed. He felt especially fortunate to be keeper of the conch because he loved the tiny but immensely powerful shell more than he had ever thought he could love anything—or anyone. Still, it had been two years since his last adventure when, along with his best friend Nisha, he had traveled hundreds of years back to the court of Nawab Najib and saved his subjects from being destroyed by an evil jinn. He had been happy to return to the Brotherhood after having completed his task, and in the last couple of years he had learned many valuable skills. But he was ready for a new quest.

Distracted by all these thoughts, he bungled the Transformation he was attempting, turning his palm leaf, quite inexplicably, into a large and extremely blue turban. His classmates snickered, and Mihirdatta stared in disbelief.

"However did you manage that? In all my years of teaching, I've never seen a student come up with that particular result. Ah, well! It's obvious that you'll be of no use until you've found out what Master Abhaydatta wants. You might as well go to him right now."

Anand bowed gratefully, handed the turban to the apprentice next to him, and hurried to the door, almost tripping over a stool in the process. Mihirdatta shook his head, but Anand noticed a small smile playing on his lips as though he hadn't forgotten what it was to be young and hungry for heroic exploits.

Anand ran all the way to the Hall of Seeing, a small, elegant building formed entirely out of intertwining trees with shining green-gray leaves. Pausing at the threshold to catch his breath, he could hear the murmur of voices inside. He had arrived too early—Abhaydatta was still in conversation with someone. He was about to move away to the other side of the path when he heard his name mentioned.

"Are you sure Anand is ready for such a challenge?" a man's voice said. "He hasn't completed his fourth year of studies yet. He doesn't know the major protective chants, or the—"

With a start Anand recognized the voice as belonging to the Chief Healer, Somdatta. Whatever task Abhaydatta had planned for Anand was obviously important enough for the Chief Healer to take an interest in it! He knew he should not eavesdrop, but he couldn't resist. He hoped that his mentor, whom he idolized, would proclaim his faith in his apprentice's abilities. Abhaydatta, however, said something quite different.

"I'm not certain that he is ready, either," he replied in a

somber voice. "But some instinct I can't explain is urging me to send him forth. I fear that if I don't do it now, we may all regret it."

"I trust your wisdom, Master Abhaydatta," Somdatta replied, though he did not sound too happy. "You have my consent."

Hearing their footsteps, Anand retreated hastily. By the time the two men emerged from the building, he was hurrying up the path that bordered the lake of silver lotuses as though he had just arrived. Both healers nodded graciously to acknowledge his greeting, though Abhaydatta shot him a sharp glance from under his thick white eyebrows.

Once inside the building, the Master Healer did not waste time. "Some time ago I told you about the hermit who lives high up in the mountains, and about how one day you might study with him," he said. "Well, that time has arrived. I want you to meet him—or rather, attempt to do so, because ultimately only the hermit decides whom he will meet."

Anand remembered that distant conversation, for he had thought of it longingly from time to time. Abhaydatta had said that the hermit was the only one who knew how to develop Anand's special gift, something no one else in the Brotherhood had: his ability to communicate with objects of power. This special ability had allowed Anand to develop a unique friendship with the conch. It had also enabled him to find the Mirror of Fire and Dreaming, without which he could not have traveled back to Nawab Najib's court. With the help of the hermit, who knew how many other objects of power he might learn to work with! His heart leaped at the thought.

Abhaydatta smiled wryly. "Don't get too excited! It's quite uncomfortable on the mountain, and the hermit can be capricious. You may not see him at all. But I'll do what I can to help you. I'll give you directions to a cave that he uses from time to time, and I'll equip you with gifts that I think he'll like. You'll carry enough food and drink for three days. If he doesn't come to you by then, you must return to the Brotherhood. This is important! As you no doubt heard when you were eavesdropping"—here he turned a stern gaze on Anand, making him squirm—"the mountain is dangerous. I'll weave a protection around you, but it will last only three days. After that, you'll become easy prey for the forces that dwell there."

Anand started to ask about these forces, but Abhaydatta stopped him with a raised hand. "You must tell no one about your coming journey. Even with the best of intentions, boys aren't necessarily as discreet as they might be, and the news might reach the wrong ears."

"Can't I tell Nisha?" Anand asked, dismayed at the thought of keeping such an important secret from the girl who was his best friend and confidante. She had shared his adventures since the time he had been a twelve-year-old living in the slums of Kolkata and she an orphaned sweeper girl.

Abhaydatta closed his eyes and thought for a moment, his eyes darting side to side beneath their lids as though he was reading something. "You may mention it to her," he said finally, though he didn't explain why.

With quick strokes, using only a fingertip that left a sparkly trail on the floor of the hall, Abhaydatta drew a map of the path that would lead Anand to the cave. He made Anand pronounce carefully the password he would have to use to get back into the valley, for its boundaries were always kept magically sealed against intruders. Then he went on to explain the complicated protocols of visiting a hermit: how to bow to him, how to address him, how to offer him gifts, and what questions not to ask him under any circumstances. Anand had no opportunity to inquire about the dangers that lurked on the mountain. But as he hurried to his next task of the day, he thought, perhaps that was for the best.

At dinner that night Anand made sure to sit next to Nisha. As he quietly told her about his upcoming task, she gave a sigh of envy, pushing back the unruly hair that framed her face.

"How I'd love to go up there with you! But Mother Amita would have a fit if I even suggested it."

Nisha had a flair for exaggeration. But in this case, Anand thought, she was probably right. Mother Amita, the herbmistress to whom Nisha was apprenticed, and with whom she lived in a cottage at the far edge of the valley, had become increasingly strict as Nisha grew older. All this last year—perhaps because Nisha was the only girl in the Brotherhood—Amita kept a close eye on her, allowing her to join the other apprentices only at lessons and meals. Recently, she had insisted that instead of the tunic and pants that the boys wore, Nisha should dress in a long, shapeless skirt and a shawl that covered her hair. Anand knew that such restrictions were difficult for his free-spirited friend, but she put up with them because she loved being part of the Brotherhood, which was the only family she had ever known.

"Oh well," Nisha said, brightening. "Maybe Mother Amita will make a trip down into the gorge of herbs soon—we've almost run out of brahmi plants—and I can go with her. I love the gorge. The trees there are strangely shaped, so that they look like old people. And the birds that nest there aren't scared at all. They'll fly down and sit on your wrist if you call to them." An idea struck her, making her eyes sparkle. "Maybe I can get her to let me go by myself! Wouldn't that be exciting?"

Anand nodded, though inwardly he doubted that the cautious herbmistress would allow Nisha to go anywhere by herself.

Nisha's eyes narrowed as though she guessed what he was thinking. That did not surprise him. The two friends knew each other so well that they often seemed to read each other's minds. "Ah, but I have a secret weapon. Remember that special course we took in Persuasion a month ago from Master

Somdatta? Well, I've been practicing it—every single day!"

"But you aren't supposed to use Persuasion on our teachers!" Anand said, shocked. Somdatta had emphasized that the complex skill, which required using one's voice in a particular way while focusing attention on the subject's heart region, was to be employed only when one was in danger.

"Well," Nisha said, reading his thoughts again, "I'm in danger of losing my mind from boredom. Does that count?" She grinned at his disapproving expression and patted his hand. "Don't worry! I'll only try it once. If it doesn't work, I'll satisfy myself with trailing behind Mother Amita."

Anand smiled, remembering how impatient Nisha been when he first met her, how insistent on getting her own way. And what an inflammable temper she'd had! She still had traces of those qualities, but overall she had matured in the years since she'd joined the Brotherhood. He hoped he had grown as much, but secretly, he was skeptical. Perhaps he still lacked confidence, as when he had been a dishwasher boy at a roadside tea stall in Kolkata, taunted and slapped around by his employer. Otherwise, why did a tendril of misgiving tighten around his heart as he thought of his journey, as he remembered the Chief Healer's reluctant agreement? Why did he fear that somehow he would make a dreadful mistake?

After dinner, Anand went to bid good-bye to the conch in the Crystal Hall. Starlight shone through the transparent dome of the hall, lighting his way as he entered. As he walked to the center of the hall, where the conch was housed inside an exquisite lotus-shaped shrine, he felt calmer than he had all day.

He had hoped the hall would be empty, but as always there were people there, meditating. Fortunately—though it wasn't as satisfying—Anand could speak to the conch silently and hear its answers inside his head. Standing close to the shrine, he told it about his upcoming journey, though he did not bother to explain the details. He knew from experience that the conch had its own way of finding out whatever it wished to know. He did, however—somewhat hesitantly, for the conch could be quite caustic on occasion—confide his doubts to it.

The conch was unusually serious in its reply.

It is quite natural that you're anxious. Even apprentices far senior to you would have quailed at the thought of spending three days alone on the mountain, which is a place of ancient enchantments. Abhaydatta has set you a challenging task—but he would not have done so if he didn't trust you. You, too, must trust yourself, for that—and not the spells the Brotherhood teaches you—is the strongest weapon you have.

What if I fail? Anand asked. *What if the hermit doesn't like me or decides I'm not worth talking to?*

There is nothing to be done if that happens, is there? But that is not what failure is.

It isn't?

No. Listen carefully, because one day soon you will have to put this lesson into practice. If you grow dejected about what comes to you, that is failure. If you accept it serenely and do what is needful, that is success. Now you must rest—but before you go, you may hold me, if you like. We will be apart for quite a while, after all.

Anand was surprised at the offer because the conch rarely expressed its affection for him. But he wasn't going to turn down this rare opportunity! Though his job as keeper required him to clean the shrine each day, he handled the conch only once a year, when it received its ritual bath. At that time the Chief Healer would unlock the shrine with the requisite chants in front of a hall full of people. It was a stately affair, but by no means an intimate experience.

Glancing around to make sure no one was looking, he extended his hand toward the shrine. When his fingers touched the crystal wall, it melted to allow his hand through. He picked up the conch carefully and brought it to his chest, feeling it pulse against his heart. How light it was, how seemingly fragile! Looking at it, so like a common shell one might find on any beach, who could guess at its power? A crack ran along one of its sides. As Anand ran his finger along it, he was overwhelmed with gratitude—and sorrow—for it was in a battle to save Anand from the jinn that the conch had sustained this injury.

Now, now, said the conch in its usual wry tone. *Don't go all maudlin on me.*

Anand smiled as he replaced the conch. But at the door of the hall he paused, struck by something it had said. *What did you mean by* we will be apart for quite a while? he asked. *I'm only going away for three nights.*

Was it his imagination, or was there the slightest of pauses before the conch's answer?

You mean three nights away from me doesn't seem like a long while to you? I'm insulted!

Sitting at the cold, uncomfortable cave entrance, Anand thought the conch had been right. Three nights—no four—on this desolate mountainside away from it was a very long while. It was time he went home.

How excited he had been the first day when he reached the cave! Though the climb had been strenuous, he could not sit still. He kept stepping outside the cave and walking around, swinging his arms in exaggerated arcs, hoping that the movements would catch the hermit's attention, wherever he might be. All that night, he barely slept. What if the hermit chose to drop in on him in the silent hours before dawn? Anand didn't want him to think that he was shirking his duty. But it had been for nothing.

By the third day, Anand's spirits had sunk. Keeping Abhaydatta's warning in mind, he'd gathered up his things, resigned to returning to the valley. But when he stepped outside, he discovered, not far from the entrance, a footprint in the snow. Had the hermit approached the cave? Was this a sign that he was about to grant Anand a meeting? Anand was torn. He hated to disobey Abhaydatta. And yet it seemed that he was very close to his goal. How could he bear to give up now? He decided to stay one more night. Surely his mentor wouldn't want him to quit just when success approached his grasp. And what could happen to him—especially if he stayed inside the cave—for just a few more hours?

But it had been a waste of time. Now, no doubt, he would be punished for having disobeyed Abhaydatta.

Anand picked up the twin staffs that he would need to maneuver his way down the steep, icy slope. He considered taking back the bag Abhaydatta had packed with dried fruit and nuts and warm woolen robes for the hermit. It would serve the man right for not showing up, he thought, and for tantalizing him with that footprint. But at the last moment he dropped it in a corner of the cave and blew out the lamp.

Coming up to the cave had been difficult, but going down, Anand discovered, was even more challenging. The trail was narrow and at times disappeared completely, forcing him to clamber over jagged rocks. Luckily, on the way up, following the healer's instructions, he had hammered colored stakes into the ground at regular intervals. He followed these now. But surely he'd used more stakes! Where had the others disappeared to, leaving him with large gaps on the path that made him wonder if he was going the right way? Several times his feet slid on the treacherous moraine that lined the mountainside, and he had to dig his staffs in hard to avoid slipping over the edge. Who knew how far he would tumble if he lost his footing! This high up, there were no bushes to break his fall. Once, looking down, he saw all the way into a dark, hungry gorge that must have been a thousand feet below. It seemed to beckon to him. With a shudder, he turned his eyes from it.

After a while, the trail wound around to the other side of the peak. Anand heaved a sigh of relief. From what he remembered, now the trail would widen. He would also be able to see the Silver Valley. Though it was still several hours away, even a distant glimpse of his beloved home would give him strength. He hurried to the edge for a look, eager to see which of the buildings he could recognize.

There was nothing below except a barren stretch of rock and snow.

Anand blinked, then rubbed his eyes. He was tired. That must be it! But when he looked again, there was still nothing. His heart began to pound. Was the mountain playing a trick on him? Had he lost his way? Maybe he needed to go around farther to the other side. But in that direction his path was blocked by a gigantic black rock. Besides, he could see the trail quite clearly, wending its way below, its edges marked, from time to time, by the colored dots of his stakes.

He took a deep breath to calm himself. Of course! The valley had a spell laid over it to keep it safe from outsiders. That must be why he couldn't see any of its buildings or pastures. How foolish he had been to panic! How Nisha would laugh at him if she knew! Still, a sense of unease clung to him. He hurried down the path, going too fast now, tripping over stones. By the time he came to the two upright, gatelike rocks where he had started his journey, his robe was torn and his arms were lacerated. He paid no attention to the pain. Standing before the rocks on the spot he had marked with the first of his stakes, his voice shaking, he spoke the password that would make the rocks slide aside, granting him entry.

Nothing happened.

And yet something was different. When he had left the valley, Anand had heard Abhaydatta speak the words to close the doorway. He had seen the rocks come together until not even a hairline gap was left between them. But now, even before he had pronounced the password, there was enough space between them for a boy to squeeze through.

Anand moved forward tentatively, his hand held out in front of him. Sometimes gateways were protected by energy instead of a physical barrier. But he felt no tingling, no elasticity in the air pressing back against his palm. The door was unguarded!

His mouth dry with fear, Anand pushed his way through the gap. The sight that met his eyes on the other side evaporated his last hope. Where earlier there had been a flower-lined pathway that led past the dormitories and mango orchards, now there were only craggy rocks covered with ice. There weren't even any ruins to show what had once stood here.

Anand couldn't stop shaking—and it had nothing to do with the freezing temperature around him. What had happened in the four days since he had been gone? Where had everyone disappeared? What had become of his beloved conch? Or—and this was the worst of the thoughts that swirled in his brain—had there never been anything here? Had he, out of some desperate desire, dreamed it all?

That was when he heard the sound of crying.

He ran toward the source of the noise, thanking the Powers that there was some other life in this desolate place. To his surprise, he found Nisha slumped next to a rock, face hidden in her hands, body racked by sobs. Next to her was a spilled basket of herbs. He touched her shoulder tentatively, not quite daring to believe that it was her. She started, thrusting out the small knife she used for herb cutting, but when she recognized him, the knife fell from her hands and she clutched his arms gratefully.

"Thank God you're here, Anand! I thought I'd gone mad!"

"I was thinking the same thing," Anand said, feeling equally thankful to have found his friend.

"How can everything disappear like this, without leaving the slightest trace?" Nisha's voice rose in agitation.

"I don't know," Anand said. "But how did you escape whatever happened to everyone else here?"

"I must have used Persuasion really well—or maybe I just wore out Mother Amita with my pestering. Yesterday she had Master Abhaydatta weave me a spell of protection and sent me down to the gorge to fetch some herbs. I got back about an hour ago. How I wish I hadn't insisted on going! Wherever the rest of the Brotherhood are, that's where I want to be, too!" She burst into tears again.

"Don't say that!" Anand implored, his heart twisting because Nisha never cried. "Otherwise I'd be all alone now. We'll try to find out what happened, but first we must take care of ourselves. I'm starving—and you must be, too. Do you have any food or water?"

Nisha shook her head. "Mother Amita gave me only enough to eat on the way down, because the gorge has a spring and many fruit trees. But it's too far away. We'll never reach it before dark. And it's getting so cold and windy."

"We'll go to the hermit's cave," Anand said, trying to sound more confident than he felt. "The path is steep, but I'll give you one of my staffs. Abhaydatta had packed me food and clothing for the hermit. I left them there. We can use those, and the cave will shelter us. Tomorrow we'll decide on a plan."

Chilled, hungry, disheartened, and acutely aware that they were no longer protected from the dangers of the mountain, the two friends started the long, hard climb.

THE HERMIT'S CAVE

The sun was setting. Behind Anand and Nisha, the sky had turned a beautiful purple, but they were too harried to enjoy it. More of the colored stakes had disappeared, and this had slowed them down as they climbed up, especially wherever the path forked. The absence of the markers worried Anand. Clearly there was some kind of malignant force on the mountain that did not wish them well—and the disappearance of the valley and its healers had strengthened it. He could feel it in the biting wind that had risen, a wind that hit them in sudden gusts, almost making them lose their balance. The lower the sun sank, the harder the wind grew, and the colder it became. His hands were so chilled that he could hardly feel the staff he was holding. From time to time, he heard the growl of thunder, but when he looked up, the sky was cloudless. He didn't share his misgivings with Nisha— she was nervous enough already—but when she wanted to stop and rest, he wouldn't allow it.

Nisha grew increasingly irritable as they climbed. "What a dictator you've become!" she shouted at one point. "Do you have any idea how tired I am? I've been climbing all day. I have blisters as big as tomatoes on my feet!"

Anand bit back the retort that rose to his tongue because he knew a quarrel would waste the little time and energy they had. He guessed that was exactly what the mountain wanted. Though he couldn't have explained why, he knew that it was essential that they reach the cave before dark. "Come on, Nisha. It's just a little farther!" he urged, taking her hand to pull her up a steep part of the trail.

He half expected her to snatch her hand away. But she must have been truly exhausted, because she allowed him to assist her.

"Do you hear something?" she whispered. "It's like an animal panting."

Anand listened, but he could not hear anything above the wind's eerie whine and the strange growling sounds. But he had a distinct feeling that something was following them, and that darkness would increase its powers. He tried to run, pulling Nisha along. The mouth of the cave was only a few feet ahead. But at that moment the sun dipped behind a peak. As though in response, the ground turned slippery as glass under their feet. It was impossible to dig their staffs into its smooth, hard surface. To stop themselves from sliding backward, they had to fall to their knees.

Now Anand could hear the panting Nisha had mentioned. As the wind swirled around him, a rotting stench assaulted his nose. Although he knew he should not, he couldn't help looking over his shoulder. In the failing evening light, some-thing immense was gliding up the hill. He could not see what it was, for a black fog surrounded it. But he could feel its malevolence, and its hunger.

He wrenched his attention from it—and from his own fear—and directed it to the glassy ground. He tried to remember what he had learned of Transformation and apply it to the path. "Be as you were before!" he whispered to it as he tried to reach its essence. He could almost feel it, layers of light that were overlaid by a black sheet. He tried to push the sheet away. As though from afar, he could hear Nisha's voice crying, "Stop! Come no closer!" She was trying to use Persuasion on the creature that followed them. It gave a growl of annoyance, the way a lion might growl at a mouse, but the fog paused, if only for a moment.

Perhaps the Transformation skill had worked a little, too, for Anand's fingers found a rock to the side of the road— and then another. Holding on to these and using all their strength, the two of them were able to drag themselves up the slope, one arm's length at a time until somehow they managed to reach the cave. Behind them they heard a howl. A rush of fetid air launched itself at the cave. Anand and Nisha shrank back in terror, but whatever had stalked them was unable to pass through the cave mouth. It didn't go away, though. They could hear it pacing outside. It knew it could wait them out. For the moment, however, they were safe.

Inside the cave, it was pitch-black and not much warmer than outside. With numb fingers Anand groped around for the lamp, but he could not locate it. Nor could he find the bag.

"I can't understand where they could have gone," he exclaimed.

"Maybe the hermit came by afterward and took them," Nisha suggested from the other side of the cave. She sounded as though she, too, was on her knees, searching.

The thought that the hermit had been nearby, watching until he left, was a bitter one for Anand. Angry words rose to his lips, but right then Nisha gave a scream. "There's someone here! I touched a foot. Help! It's got me!"

Anand's heart jolted with fear. So much for his belief that they would be safe in the cave!

"I'm coming, Nisha!" he shouted, running toward his friend's voice. But in the dark he tripped on a rock and went flying. His breath knocked out of him, he came to a stop against—yes, it was a bare, hairy foot!

"Good grief!" boomed a voice. "How many of you little pests *are* there?" A hard, bony hand grabbed Anand's shoulder and pulled him up. There was the sound of a flint being struck.

In the hazy lamplight that filtered through the cave, Anand saw a tall, thin man looming over Nisha and himself. He was clothed in a brand-new woolen robe that was much too loose for him. Unruly hair radiated from his head in every direction. His eyes glittered in the lamplight, but the look in them, though exasperated, was not unkind.

"You're the hermit!" Anand croaked.

The hermit did not bother responding to this observation, nor did he ask what they were doing in his cave. He strode off to a dark corner, where he busied himself, with much muttering, with something Anand couldn't see.

"Do you think we could ask him for something to eat?" Nisha whispered in Anand's ear. "There must be *some* food left in the bag that Abhaydatta sent."

"Of course there is!" The voice echoed against the cave walls. "I'm a hermit, not a bottomless pit. That's what I was working on, Miss Impatience, in addition to keeping the yaksha that was stalking you from entering the cave."

Anand saw the hermit approach them, two earthen bowls in his hands. One held the dried fruits and nuts that Abhaydatta had packed, along with a bunch of ripe bananas. The other, to Anand's surprise, held fresh milk.

"The monkeys bring me fruit from the gorges, and the milk is from the wild goats that share the mountain with me." The hermit grinned, tickled by the boy's surprise. "You'll have to tell young Abhaydatta when you see him next that he shouldn't worry about my meals."

Young Abhaydatta? Anand thought. How old was this hermit that he could refer to his mentor in this manner? Along with that came another thought: Where was the healer now?

The hermit held out the bowls. "Go on!" he said.

Anand and Nisha didn't need a second invitation. With a hurried word of thanks, they divided the food between them and finished it most efficiently. While they ate, the hermit disappeared into the darkness of the cave. This time he returned with blankets and a stack of wood. In a few moments he had a fire blazing. Gratefully, the two friends drew close to it, wrapping themselves in the blankets the hermit tossed their way.

The hermit sat facing them, his body still as the rocks that made up the cave. Only his sharp, hooded eyes flickered as he scrutinized their faces. Anand had the uncomfortable feeling that the hermit was looking deep into their hearts. Anand's face grew hot as he remembered how many names he'd called the hermit for not showing up. Would the hermit hold that against him? Would he refuse to help them? He tried to find the right words to apologize, but they wouldn't come.

Fortunately, Nisha spoke up, direct as ever. "As you can see, we're in a lot of trouble. Our home's destroyed, and our teachers have vanished. Do you know what happened?"

The hermit took his time to answer.

"Some things I know," he finally said, "and some I can only guess. The force that has turned the valley into this frozen wasteland came from a distant world, too far away for me to gauge its nature. I felt it circling the valley for the last several days, but I did not know what it was searching for. Now I see that it wanted to find objects of power. Perhaps Abhaydatta sensed it, too. Maybe that's why he sent you"—he nodded at Anand—"up to me. That was also why I didn't come to the cave and instead tempted you with a footprint when you were about to leave. I wanted to keep you up here, where you would be safe."

Anand lowered his eyes, ashamed. How mistaken he'd been, jumping to conclusions, thinking the worst of the hermit! The next time, he promised himself, he wouldn't judge someone so quickly.

The hermit smiled as though he knew Anand's thoughts. Then he continued, "When the force sensed the conch, it focused all its power on it and pulled it through the abyss that underlies time and space into its own world. Once the conch was gone from our world, none of the things that depended on its presence could continue. That's why the buildings disappeared, and the fields, and the parijat trees." Here the hermit gave a sigh. "Ah, those trees were pretty! It cheered me to look down on their silver blossoms."

"What happened to the Brotherhood?" Nisha blurted out.

"I'm not sure. The healers most adept in magic were probably pulled into the other world with the conch. The others may be stuck in the abyss. Poor souls!"

Anand remembered his first time in the abyss, when he'd lost both the conch and Nisha in its violent, black whirling. He shuddered, imagining how terrifying it must be to be caught in that whirling forever, not knowing what had occurred.

"Can't you do something to help them?" he asked.

The hermit shook his head. "I relinquished all such skills a long time ago, when I chose the meditative life. There's only one remedy to this problem. Someone must go into the other world and retrieve the conch, which has the power to set things right by its mere presence. Perhaps the two of you can do it."

"Us?" Anand cried, aghast. "By ourselves?"

The hermit nodded. "You have reserves that run deep, though you are not aware of them yet. And the healers have taught you many skills."

Anand wasn't convinced. But before he could express his doubts, Nisha said, "Without the conch to open a portal for us, how can we travel to another world?"

"That is a problem," the hermit admitted. "Is there perhaps another object of power to which you have access?"

Anand stared into the firelight, thinking hard. The objects of power that had been there in the valley had all disappeared with the conch. Probably there were other such objects hidden in the everyday world of the cities, but he did not know how to find them.

As he blew out his breath in a great, disheartened sigh, the orange flames leaped up. He thought he saw a flash at the heart of the fire. It looked like a small square of glass. And, just like that, he remembered the Mirror of Fire and

Dreaming. After defeating the jinn, Anand had left the mirror in the care of the Nawab's son. But the mirror had promised to come to Anand's aid if he needed it again.

What could be a greater need than this?

Excited, he turned to Nisha. "We'll ask the mirror to help us," he said.

Nisha's eyes lost some of their worry. To the hermit, who was looking at them questioningly, she explained, "Not only can this mirror take you to any place you need to visit, but it can also get you into buildings that may be heavily guarded. That's how we got into the Nawab's treasure house the last time and rescued the conch."

"It is the perfect object, then, and you are fortunate to have its friendship," said the hermit. "I'll add my mental energy to your invitation." He sprinkled a handful of dust onto the fire—but perhaps it wasn't dust, for it made the flames turn a deep pomegranate color—and took their hands in his gaunt ones.

Sitting in a circle, hands clasped, the three of them closed their eyes and focused. Anand couldn't quite remember what the mirror looked like, but he did remember how it had felt in his hands, hot and throbbing and heavier than normal as it showed him scenes from another time. He focused on that feeling and used Search, a skill that fashioned his mental energy into the shape of an arrow, and launched it into space.

Anand wasn't sure how much time had passed since he had closed his eyes. His head ached with effort. A Search arrow was supposed to be able to find whatever a healer was looking for and communicate the healer's thoughts to it. But Anand had never tried to use Search to reach another period of time. Was it even possible? He was about to give up when, to his excitement, he felt words forming in his mind.

Anand! Why do you call me?

In response Anand sent out an image of the devastated valley. *We need you to take us to the conch,* he added. *You're our only hope.*

The answer floated back to Anand, gracious in its simplicity. *Then I will come.*

Anand opened his eyes. Before he could explain to his companions what had taken place, there was a crash, along with a fountain of light. A shining square of about three handspans appeared on the floor of the cave. It was the mirror.

The hermit looked at it with great interest. "I do believe this is one of the three looking glasses forged in the Age of Truth from the sands of the Great Northern Desert." Closing his eyes, he held the mirror in his hands for a while. Then he said, "I have told it all I know of the world into which you must go. Find the conch and return as soon as you can. Most importantly, do not get involved in the events of that world, be they good or bad. And hurry. Right now the shape of the valley, being new, is malleable. I can help keep it so—

but not for long. In seven days, the universe will harden itself around this new shape. Then even the conch might not be able to restore it."

Nisha—always intrepid—was the first to approach the shining square. She bowed to the mirror, and then turned to Anand, eyes dancing at the possibility of a new adventure. "I, for one, am ready to leave this dreary place!" she said, placing her feet squarely on the mirror.

Just as she disappeared with a flash, Anand heard the hermit laugh. At the sound, a strange foreboding filled him. Did the hermit laugh because the world into which the mirror would plunge them was far worse than this present moment on the chill mountainside? What kind of creatures inhabited this world? How powerful they must have been, to pull the conch from its home! How could Anand hope to wrest the conch from their grasp? But there was no time to hesitate. He stepped onto the mirror and felt its cool smoothness through the soles of his shoes. A burst of light dazzled him, and he felt himself tumbling with amazing speed into the abyss that lies beneath the dimensions.

SHADOWLAND

Anand landed on his back on a rough surface, the breath knocked out of him. He sat up, shaking his dazed head. The journey through the abyss—different each time—had felt like he was being spun in one of the mixie-machines his mother had described to him when she worked as a maid in a rich man's house. He took a deep breath to clear his head, but this only made him feel worse. That was when he noticed the brownness. It was all around him: on the cracked pavement where he had landed, on the walls of the gutted buildings, on the metal poles that looked like lampposts but were much taller—and in the air. Was he in the midst of a dust storm? Was it smoke of some kind? But when he looked around, he realized that the brownness was even and stretched as far as the eye could see, obscuring the sky so that he could not tell what time of day it was. He realized with a shock that in the world to which the conch had been pulled, the air had turned brown. It had a strange, scorched smell to it and scraped his throat as he breathed, making him want to retch. Nisha, who had landed near him, scrunched up her nose and coughed.

"The air tastes funny, like rusted metal," she whispered. "And everything is—faded. Are we in Shadowland?"

Anand shivered. According to the books of lore they had studied, Shadowland was the world occupied by the restless spirits of those who had met violent ends. He knew it couldn't be. The dead had no need of the conch's powers. Still, he felt deeply uneasy.

Nisha was dressed in a baggy brown bodysuit that extended from her neck all the way to her feet. It looked like a uniform of some kind. Glancing down, Anand saw that he was similarly clothed. He knew from earlier experience that the mirror had the ability to change people's appearance to fit the world to which it transported them, and he wondered who he was supposed to be here.

Anand peered around to see what other people (if indeed people inhabited this world) were wearing, and how they dealt with the rusty air that was getting increasingly hard to breathe. But the alleyway in which he found himself was completely empty. With a little shiver, he realized that they were in a bad part of town. Piles of garbage were heaped against large buildings that looked like abandoned warehouses or apartment complexes. Graffiti— strange, tantalizing red scrawls that Anand could almost decipher—disfigured their walls. As he stared at them, he heard the sound of an approaching siren, a high-pitched, nerve-racking sound he recognized from his old life in

Kolkata. Some things, at least, were no different here.

"Someone is in trouble—or about to get into it," he rasped to Nisha. "We'd better find a hiding place." She nodded. As a street child, she knew that the farther one stayed from the authorities, the better. But as Anand glanced around for a sanctuary, she pulled at something around his neck.

"What's this?"

He looked down. It was an assortment of tubes, one end of which disappeared into the suit. The other opened into a bowl-like structure with an elastic band attached to its rim.

"Maybe it goes over your nose and mouth," he guessed. Nisha's suit had the same tubed attachments. They pulled the bowls over their faces.

"Ah! It's a lot easier to breathe now," Nisha said thankfully. From inside the bowl, her voice sounded distorted, mechanical. But Anand had no chance to remark on this— nor on a quick movement he'd caught, out of the corner of his eye, near an abandoned building—because the sirens had suddenly grown very loud. They sounded as if they were directly overhead. Looking up, he saw that high above them ran a crisscross of raised, see-through roadways, and along one of them a red bullet-shaped car was fast approaching. Strobe lights flashed from it.

"Quick!" he called, grabbing Nisha's elbow, dragging her toward the only hiding place he could think of—the nearest pile of garbage.

"Even if they see us, they can't get down here," Nisha whispered, as they ran toward a stack of furniture that looked like it had met a violent end.

But as Anand nodded agreement, he saw the bullet car lift off the road. Whirring blades, as on a helicopter, had appeared on its roof, allowing it to land right next to the young people. Two red creatures—he did not know what else to call them—jumped out, carrying what Anand suspected to be weapons: long blue tubes with tiny holes. Before Anand and Nisha could dive behind a broken sofa, the creatures had grabbed them and clapped a thin metal collar around each of their necks. Anand pulled at his, trying to tear it off, but it was immensely strong. The cold metal sent a shiver through him as he wondered what it was for.

"Take out your time and place permits," the taller of the two creatures barked. Up close, Anand could see that it was actually a man in a tight-fitting bodysuit made of a shiny red material. He wore a red mask that molded itself to his face, obscuring his features. Though he understood what the man said, Anand didn't recognize the language he spoke. But like the graffiti, it tantalized him with a sense of familiarity.

At least, he thought with a sigh of relief, he was in a world peopled by humans.

"What's a time and space permit?" Nisha asked, speaking in the same language. Obviously, the mirror had adjusted their speech as well as their appearance.

The mirror! It was still lying on the edge of the street, in the spot where they had entered this world! Anand could see it glinting faintly through the smoky air. It was a wonder that the policemen (if that was who they were) hadn't noticed it yet.

Anand knew he had to hide it. But how would he manage that?

"Don't act smart with us, girl!" the other man, who was short and burly, said. "Everyone knows what permits are." His hand shot out with startling speed to deliver a cuff to Nisha's head. But Nisha's years as a street child had been spent dodging many similar blows. She leaped back with amazing agility, and then, before the man realized what had happened, she rushed forward, barreling into him with all her might. The policeman wasn't expecting such a response. (Anand suspected that his victims were usually too cowed to attack back.) He lost his balance and landed heavily on the ground, the breath audibly knocked out of him. Yelling at Anand to follow, Nisha ran toward the nearest building, intending to jump through a broken window. But the other policeman aimed his blue cylinder at them. Anand stiffened, expecting bullets or maybe a stream of fire. He saw nothing, but a paralyzing pain wrenched his joints and he fell to the ground. Nisha had suffered the same fate. His heart beat faster as he listened to the ominous tread of approaching boots. What would happen to them now?

He was equally worried about the mirror, still lying exposed on the street. Whatever force had torn the conch from the Silver Valley would not spare the mirror if it sensed its presence. And if anything happened to the mirror, they would be trapped forever in this nightmare world.

Help me to help you! he cried silently to the mirror.

In response, a ray of light arced from the mirror to where Nisha lay. It fell on her face, lighting it up, and then seemed to travel into her. She sat up slowly, shaking her head as though emerging from underwater. When she spoke to the staring policemen, her voice was calm and very pleasant. "Please forgive my previous action, sirs. Panic made me respond in such an inappropriate manner. We come from a faraway place. We have never been in this city before. Our customs are different, so we don't know about the permits you mentioned."

Anand held his breath. Nisha was using Persuasion— but at a very high level, far beyond the capacity of even a senior apprentice. Had the mirror enhanced her skill?

The man sprawled on the ground gave an angry snort of disbelief, but the other policeman tapped his chin. "It's possible," he said to his companion. "Remember how last year we heard that one of the guards had found some people from the Outer Lands?"

"Yes!" The shorter man sat up, excited. "I heard he made a solid bundle of money from it, too, turning them in to one of the rehabitationals. Maybe we can do the same!"

"You'd better keep your hands to yourself, then," his partner responded. "Our clients don't like damaged goods."

While the men were busy conferring, Anand crawled to the mirror. He was afraid that if he took the mirror to the garbage pile to hide it, the policemen would notice him. So he picked it up and, with a whisper of apology, lobbed it onto a pile of mattresses that leaked stuffing. *Keep yourself safe until I can come back to you*, he said.

I will, came the answer. The ray of light faded.

"What was that?" said the short policeman, looking around suspiciously. "I thought I saw something shining in the sky."

"Probably another meteor shower," his companion responded. "Let's get these two to Rehabilitational 39—that's the closest one— before it hits us and collects our payment."

Anand and Nisha were herded into the backseat of the bullet car, which was fenced in by thick black bars. The windows were blacked out, so they could see nothing outside. The short policeman glowered at them as he slammed the door, but he did not attempt to hurt them. Anand guessed that the officer's newly found self-control was motivated largely by greed. As the car took off with an impatient jerk, with a sinking heart he wondered what waited for them at their destination.

✁

Anand sank down on the narrow metal cot nailed to the floor of the room into which he'd been thrust and looked around in dismay. The cot took up most of the small, low room, and Anand could barely stand up without hitting his head on the ceiling. The walls around him were made of some kind of wiry mesh. When Anand touched it, the mesh gave off an electrical charge that tingled unpleasantly all the way up his arm. Startled, he jumped back—and was further startled by the sound of laughter. At least that's what he thought it was; the sound was choked off almost immediately. Looking into the next cell—for that's what these rooms were, he realized—he saw that it held a curly-haired boy about the same age as him. He was dressed in a too-small uniform the color of mud—the same kind of clothes that Anand had been given upon being admitted into the rehabitational. The boy gestured, a series of fluid hand movements that Anand guessed was some kind of sign language.

Anand shook his head. "I don't understand," he began to say. But scarcely had he spoken the first word when a shooting pain came from the collar around his neck, making him gasp and stagger. The boy grimaced, pointing to his own neck. Anand saw that he, too, wore a similar collar. Now he understood! The collars were voice-sensitive devices, activated whenever the authorities wanted to prevent the people forced to wear them from communicating with each other. His heart sank. He desperately needed to know more about this strange world, but it was impossible.

He wasn't sure how many hours had passed since the policemen brought Nisha and him to the rehabitational, a hulking, sooty structure with no windows. Was it morning, or was it still night? It was imperative to keep track of time.

Otherwise, how would he be able to get back to the valley within a week, as the hermit had warned them to?

Upon arrival, Anand and Nisha had been herded to the Intake Department and separated from each other. There, men in black uniforms bombarded Anand with questions about his name, his tribe, his place of origin, and his reason for being in this city. He was unable to provide satisfactory answers to any of these. He wondered how Nisha was faring; he hoped that she was holding on to her temper.

At first Anand's interrogators had been angry, but then they hooked him up to a machine and decided he wasn't lying to them. They, too, came to the conclusion that he had arrived from the Outer Lands but suspected that he was suffering from memory loss, probably as a result of some trauma.

"I wonder what happened to him," one of the smaller uniforms said in a voice that was softer than the others. With a start, Anand realized that it was a woman.

The man who had led the interrogation shrugged. "Who knows? Just being here in the city of Coal is enough to traumatize anyone, especially some poor fool from the Outer Lands!" His voice turned stern. "M-4372, you know the rules: You must not show interest in any of the inmates, or get involved with them in any manner. Otherwise you won't be able to do your job—and then we might have to send *you* to the Outer Lands!" Several of the black uniforms hiccupped with laughter at the joke, but the woman seemed frightened and did not speak again.

The leader clapped his hands. "Make a note in his file: Starting tomorrow morning, he's to work on the Farm until he's requisitioned. Now put him in lockup and bring in the next one fast—I want to get home in time to catch the late-night hover-wrestling show on the Pod!"

As Anand was dragged away, he mused on the one piece of information he'd gathered: He was in a city called Coal, a city so terrible that mere exposure to it could cause a person to lose his memory.

Now Anand stared through the bars of his cell door at the huge, cavernous structure that stretched out around him. As far as he could see in the dim light, there were cells and more cells, each one occupied by a boy, each in the same mud-colored uniform, each eerily silent. Most of the boys—including the one who had earlier tried to communicate with him—were stretched out listlessly on their cots. They all wore masks. Apparently, even indoors the air was poisonous. Though he couldn't see their faces, Anand could taste the hopelessness that pervaded the entire rehabitational. He wondered what all these boys had done to end up in this dismal place. Its name, Rehabitational 39, indicated that Coal had many other facilities like this one.

Anand slumped down on his cot. His stomach churned with hunger. He hadn't had anything to eat since he had arrived in Shadowland. He wondered what kind of food was available here. He wondered how Nisha was doing. He worried about the mirror. Would it be safe? He remembered the movement he'd seen by the abandoned building. What if someone had seen the mirror? What if they took it as soon as the police left? To prevent despair from engulfing him, he closed his eyes and focused on the conch. Had it already arrived in this world? He decided to use a Search arrow to look for it. If the conch were nearby, it would surely respond.

The next moment, a flash of pain exploded in his head, so severe that he fell to the damp floor, writhing in agony. A force had repelled his search arrow, driving it back into him. Someone in this world knew about magic and was strong enough to block its use.

Anand was too disheartened to lift himself off the floor even though its chill crept into his bones. Jailed as he was, stripped of his voice and now his magic, how would he fulfill his quest?

THE FARM

A long line of boys and girls waited, sullen and silent, for breakfast in the dimly lit dining hall of the rehabitational. From the back of the line, Anand craned his neck anxiously, trying to locate Nisha. But it was impossible. The shapeless uniforms and breathing masks made everyone look alike. When he reached the servers, he was given a bowl of sloppy, gray mush made of a substance he failed to identify. It tasted like glue. Anand wanted to throw it away, but from the eagerness with which the others were tackling their bowls, he guessed that a better option would not appear any time soon. He managed to down a few spoonfuls before he gagged. When he pushed his bowl to the side, the boy next to him—the same one who had signed at him last night—gestured, asking if he could have it. Anand nodded. The boy grabbed the bowl and finished the mush in a few seconds.

Now Anand stood in another long line, under the watchful eyes of more guards, waiting to board one of the buses that would transport them to the Farm. Climbing on, he looked back one last time, not really hoping to find Nisha.

Amazingly, she wasn't too far behind, her unruly hair falling over her mask as she kicked savagely at a stone. He dared not wave. But their glances met, and it seemed a smile crinkled up her eyes. It was enough to make him feel more hopeful. With luck, she would get on the same bus. Later he would find an opportunity to communicate with her somehow, even if they could not talk.

From the outside, the bus, squat and rectangular, had looked like the vehicles Anand had seen in Kolkata, but inside it was very different. There were no seats, only rows of metal poles, crowded together. The other boys and girls had found themselves poles to hold on to, so Anand did the same. As soon as the doors of the bus shut with a whoosh, a thick belt snaked out from each pole and tightened itself around each person's waist, holding him or her effectively captive. Anand squirmed, feeling claustrophobic, but the belt did not yield. The girl standing next to him looked at him pityingly and shook her head to indicate that struggling was useless.

The walls of the bus were made of a transparent glassy material. Later Anand would learn that this was to allow passing patrol cars to check on the Illegals, as the youths who were brought to the rehabitational were termed. He stared out, hoping to discover more about this strange, troubling world. But there was nothing to see, as the rehabitational was built in the middle of a barren field where not even weeds grew. The earth here was a dirty yellow. In spite of his mask, Anand could smell the bitter odor of sulfur. He remembered the rich red earth of the fields he had tended in the Silver Valley and felt homesickness tug at his heart.

Once they started moving, though, there was plenty to observe. The bus, which was old and worn, unlike the sleek vehicles of the policemen, moaned as it climbed onto a raised roadway with many lanes. Down below lay abandoned clumps of buildings left to rot in the brown air: ruined housing complexes, market plazas, or spired structures that may have once been places of worship. But once or twice, Anand could have sworn as he peered at the collapsed roofs and crumbling walls, he saw figures darting surreptitiously from one building to another. In the distance several large spheres containing tall, imposing buildings sparkled through the brown fog. Were these the new neighborhoods and business centers of Coal? Anand wondered what kind of disaster had turned the air brown and the earth barren and driven people to retreat inside domes, but there was no way to find out.

They traveled for a long while, Anand growing increasingly restless as time passed. The moments were trickling through his hands like water, and he was no closer to finding the conch. Then the bus turned sharply onto a road that split off from the main skyway and led to a large dome. The driver identified himself to the guards at the entrance; the bus was allowed to chug through. As the Illegals descended, the sight that met Anand's eyes took his breath away.

Lush and green, the Farm was more colorful than anything he'd hoped to see in this dreary world. On one side, stretching as far as he could see were trees laden with luscious, ripe fruit. On the other lay field after field of crops. Anand could recognize rows of corn and okra. Pristine white cauliflowers of prize-winning proportions peeped through green hoods; sweet peas clambered up trellises around which bees hummed; fat yellow gourds hung from vines. Some of the cold despair left Anand's heart. The ground was carpeted with soft, dew-sprinkled grass that made him long to kick off his boots and feel the blades between his toes. Why, the people of Shadowland had created a paradise here!

A breeze carried the smell of ripe mangoes to Anand. His mouth began to water. He hoped he would be sent to the mango orchard to work. He was good at picking mangoes. He had done it often in the valley. There were so many fruits—surely the authorities wouldn't mind if he ate one or two. He looked around for Nisha, hoping they could work together. There she was, descending from the bus just ahead of the boy who had been in the cell next to Anand's. Around them, boys and girls milled around. The guards at the Farm seemed less strict than the ones at the rehabitational. Anand made use of this to surreptitiously beckon to Nisha to join him. Then he pushed his way to the front of the line, eager to get started, wondering why the others didn't seem happier to be in this beautiful place.

Ahead of them, pairs of green-uniformed guards were helping the youths remove their masks. Ah! Finally he was going to breathe some fresh air. But then Anand noticed that as one of the guards took off the masks, the other fitted a wire contraption that looked like a muzzle over their mouths. It took him a moment to grasp that it was to prevent the youths from eating anything! He exchanged a glance of dismay with Nisha. Whoever was in charge of things in Shadowland didn't care how these hungry boys and girls felt as they handled all this delicious food that was off limits for them. They thought of them only as cheap labor. How foolish he'd been to compare this place to the Silver Valley!

Still, Anand could not help but feel cheered by the profusion of color and smells around him as they were handed baskets and sent off to pick tomatoes. The tomato field was far from the guardhouse, and once they were out of sight, he grasped Nisha's hand and gave it a quick squeeze. He didn't dare activate his collar by speaking, but he hoped there would be a chance later to scratch a few sentences into the dirt. He gestured to her to accompany him to the farthest row, where they would have some privacy. Then he noticed his neighbor from last night following them. Was it his imagination, or was the boy staring at them? Anand shot him a discouraging scowl and moved quicker, dodging between rows. He needed to discuss with Nisha what they should do next, and it would ruin his plans if the boy joined them.

On reaching the far row, he purposely ignored Nisha and busied himself with picking tomatoes. In spite of his problems, he couldn't help noticing how large and juicy they were, how uniformly red, and how numerous. How had the growers managed such abundance? And why, when there was so much food available, had the youths been fed so meagerly this morning? Though he had never particularly liked tomatoes, his mouth watered as he plucked the ripe fruits and placed them in his basket. And yet, even as he fantasized about biting into a succulent tomato and feeling the juice run down his chin, something about these too-perfect fruits made him uneasy.

When his basket was almost full, Anand moved casually to the end of the row, picking up a stick as he went. Nisha, smart as ever, followed him with careful nonchalance, pausing to pluck a few more tomatoes on the way. The curly-haired boy was nowhere to be seen. Quickly, Anand hunkered down and, as concisely as he could, wrote down what had happened when he tried to use his Search skills.

I don't know what else to do to find the conch, he added, looking at Nisha for help. But she, too, seemed at a loss.

"Why don't you try again? Maybe here at the Farm you'll get through. It's quite far away from the Blocking Towers."

Anand whirled around, as astonished at the sound of a human voice as at the words. Crouched behind a tomato plant, the curly-haired boy was peering at them.

"Don't worry!" he said when he saw Anand's fearful expression. "I won't give you away."

"You can talk?" Anand whispered, speaking with difficulty through the wire mesh over his mouth.

The boy nodded. "We've found out that in some parts of the Farm the collars don't work. We don't let the guards know this, of course! Maybe it's because of the filter they've put in to keep the radioactive rays away from the food that's grown in here. It wouldn't do if the leaders of Coal—they're the only ones who get to eat this stuff—fell sick from radiation, would it?" He smiled bitterly. "Of course, no one knows what kind of long-term effect the 'enhanced' fertilizers they use on the vegetables will have on their bodies." He spat on the ground. "I hope they all shrivel up and die."

Enhanced fertilizers! Now Anand realized why everything that grew here was so oversized, why it seemed a little fake.

"What's your name?" Nisha asked. "And why did they put you in jail?"

"I'm Bas—uh, B-1112," the boy said. "They imprisoned me because I'm a magician—an apprentice, actually. They caught me while our group was on a mission. I'll tell you more later. Try your Search power before someone else shows up. You can't trust all the kids. Some of them are spies for the guards."

Without wasting any more time, Anand closed his eyes, focusing on the conch. He recalled how perfectly it fit into the palm of his hand, how it would send warmth and joy billowing through him. He remembered how a blast from it had saved his life when he battled Surabhanu the sorcerer, and how it had forced the evil jinn that threatened the Nawab's court into the Great Void. Now it was in trouble, and it was Anand's turn to rescue it.

If you've arrived in this strange world already, he cried in his mind, *then give me a sign.*

This time he could sense his Thought energy arcing over the dome like arrows, speeding in different directions. Almost immediately he recognized the conch's unmistakable voice, though it was very faint. *Locked in vault. Suffocating. Come soon. Great danger. Use scientist woman.* It faded before Anand could figure out from which direction it had come.

The boy was watching him, his eyes sharp and intense in his thin face. Could he be trusted? What if he was one of those spies he'd mentioned?

"You're a magician, too, aren't you?" the boy whispered. He made the same gesture again as last night and waited expectantly.

Anand realized that the boy wanted him to make a complementary gesture, but he did not know the right response.

"Nisha and I *are* magicians—or at least we're apprentices—but from a different world," he whispered back.

He hadn't expected the boy to believe him, but his eyes lit up. "Then the tales my grandfather, Chief Deep—uh, D-91—told me are true! Many parallel worlds exist, and in worlds where magic is stronger, interworld travel is possible. And these worlds still have objects of power."

"What do you mean, *where magic is stronger?*" Nisha demanded. "What's wrong with magic here? And surely you magicians still have objects of power?"

"Magicians in our world have been getting weaker and

weaker ever since the Great Divide, when they had a huge falling out with the scientists. Before that, our people were rich and powerful. But one day the scientists turned on us and took over the council that ruled the city. They raided our houses and took away our objects of power and destroyed our academies. They captured many of our leaders and executed them as traitors to Coal. The surviving magicians were forced to go underground. Now we live hidden among the poorest of the poor in the slums of Co—"

"Wait!" Anand interrupted. "You said *scientists*! That's what the conch mentioned, too." Quickly he explained to the boy what the conch was, what had happened to it, and why he and Nisha were here. "The conch said I had to use a woman scientist to get to the vault, where it's locked up—"

The boy wrinkled his forehead. "I don't know who it could be. There are several important women scientists in Coal. But I'd bet anything that the vault is located in the lab inside Futuredome. That's where they run all the big experiments. No one can get in there, though, unless they have special clearance. There are guards everywhere—and they're a hundred times worse than the guards at the rehabitational! I know—they're the ones that caught us when we were on our mission."

"What kind of mission?" Nisha asked.

"We were trying to destroy their converters, machines they use to create enough energy to run the Blocking Towers. The towers—you felt their effect when you tried the Search inside the rehabitational—prevent magicians from using our mind power, which is about the only weapon we have left. We got into the dome, and then inside the lab, and made it as far as their most powerful machine, the X-Converter. But someone must have tipped them off, because a whole battalion of guards arrived before we could explode the converter. We damaged it, but not enough. We fought the guards, but their tubeguns were too strong for our homemade weapons." Despair and anger darkened B's face at the memory. "They killed some of the men, and put the rest into the adult prisons. The boys and girls ended up in the rehabitationals. I've been here for almost a month, providing them with slave labor. I don't know if they'll ever let us go." He looked down, scuffing the ground with his toe. "My grandfather—he was sick when I left. And my mother—I know how much she must be worrying about me." His voice broke, and he turned away from them.

"Don't lose heart," Nisha said. "Maybe we can figure out a way to escape."

B shook his head. "I've never heard of anyone escaping from a rehabitational."

"But we *have* to get out!" Anand cried. "We have only a few days to rescue the conch. If we fail, everyone in the Silver Valley is doomed."

"The two of you may get lucky because you don't have any criminal records," B said. "The rehabitational authorities will try to rent you out to one of their wealthy patrons—

maybe as early as tomorrow. People are always coming to them looking for servants. And youths without records are in high demand because they're inexperienced and don't cause trouble for their employers—unlike the rest of us." Here he gave a fierce grin.

"I see a guard coming," Nisha interrupted.

B ducked back under the tomatoes. "I'd better go. If they see me with you, it'll cause problems for all of us. If you do get hired, run away from your employer as soon as you can. The private homes don't have as much security as the prisons."

"If we get out, I'll try to bring you help," Anand said.

B's voice came to him faintly from the other side. "Thank you. But that's too dangerous. You have your own mission to accomplish. Just destroy as many of the scientists' machines as you can. They're the root of all our problems. And if you need help after you escape, look for a shop in the old part of the city—it's called the House of Fine Spirits."

Anand wanted to ask what he would find there, but there was no more time for questions. He could hear the heavy tread of the guards' boots and their shouts as they ordered the youths to take their baskets to the cleaning shed. In the distance, he saw a guard cuffing one of the boys who hadn't managed to fill his basket. He hurried to gather more tomatoes before he met the same fate.

The rest of the day, he was kept busy picking more vegetables—bright purple brinjals with thorns that had to be handled gingerly, and pearly white onions that had to be coaxed from the ground with their stalks intact. Anand's head whirled with all the disturbing things he had learned from B-1112. He realized that that was not the boy's real name, which he had chosen to keep secret. Anand understood that impulse. One of the first things that apprentices were taught in the Silver Valley was to keep their true names secret from all except the most trusted friends. A person's true name was connected to his or her deepest being. Merely by knowing it, an enemy could gain power over the person.

Anand would have loved to ask Nisha what she thought of the war between the scientists and the magicians, but they did not get another opportunity to be by themselves. After a brief lunch of soup that was almost as tasteless as the morning's meal, they were made to work in the rice paddies, crouching in water that came up to their ankles to plant seedlings, and then, when an exhausted Anand was hoping for some rest, they were sent to the packing shed. As he washed and dried the luscious produce and arranged them in pretty baskets to be consumed by some rich and unthinking councilman, Anand used the last of his strength to cautiously send out another Search arrow. This one was directed at their potential rescuer, someone who could get them out of the rehabitational and to the conch. *Come quickly*, it entreated.

SCIENTISTS

Anand was awakened from uneasy sleep by a dig in the ribs with a tubegun. The guard at the other end of the gun yelled at him to hurry and clean himself up. He needed to be in the Showroom in exactly five minutes. Muscles still aching from yesterday's labor, Anand stumbled groggily into the showering area where, along with several other boys, he stripped and was sprayed with a stinging black liquid soap. He washed it off the best he could, shivering under the jet of cold water sprayed by a different machine, then dressed once again in an ill-fitting uniform that was tossed at him. Guards herded the boys to a large room filled with other Illegals, snatched off their masks, and locked them in without further explanation.

The room was empty except for a set of bleachers on which everyone was sitting, and several vents that noisily pumped in air. Anand scanned the faces anxiously, relaxing only when he found Nisha's. She sat on the top row of the bleachers, and though there wasn't much space, he climbed up and squeezed himself in beside her. Only then did he notice that the bleachers faced a large glass wall. He couldn't see through it, but he had a feeling that they were being watched. Around him, the youths who were veterans of the rehabitational—including B—were sitting up attentively, hiding their dispiritedness and making an effort to smile. Anand could think of only one reason why they'd do that: From the other side of the glass, prospective employers were observing them. Now he understood why their masks had been removed.

Anand's heart beat unevenly. He tried to make himself look docile and contented. Although he did not dare to use his mental powers, he wished as hard as he could that Nisha and he would be chosen. Once before, when he had been a poor boy washing dishes in the slums of Kolkata, wishing had helped change his life, bringing him in touch with Master Abhaydatta and the Silver Valley. Maybe it would work again.

Soon afterward, two guards ushered them single file to the room next door where a rehabitational officer was speaking to half a dozen men and one woman. The men were plump and prosperous-looking and were dressed in elaborately embroidered, silken uniforms decorated with braids and medals. The official must have said something funny, for they burst into laughter just as Anand entered. But the woman, who wore a simple white bodysuit, looked impatient. With her spectacles and her creased brow and her hair pulled back in a no-nonsense bun, she seemed to be all business.

One by one, the youths were instructed to stand in front of a machine that took up one side of the room. The machine would shine a ray of light into their eyes and beep in a particular tone. Then lines of information would flash on its screen. Anand guessed this to be the person's criminal record. The employers would examine it closely, make notes on pads they carried, then shake their heads or give a nod. The rejected youths were taken back to their cells, their shoulders drooping. The lucky ones who received a nod were sent to the back of the room to wait anxiously for the employers to make their final selection.

When B approached the machine, it went wild, clanging and flashing. An entire screenful of data appeared, several areas highlighted in red. The clients looked annoyed, and the woman exclaimed, with some asperity, "Don't you know by now that we never hire magicians? You shouldn't waste our time with the likes of him." The official apologized profusely at the oversight and barked at the guards, one of whom grabbed B roughly by the arm and dragged him away. Anand hoped they wouldn't hurt him. But he did not have too much time to worry about B, because now it was his turn to approach the machine.

When Anand stood in front of it, the machine made a soft chittering sound and the screen remained blank. The employers were most intrigued by this development, whispering excitedly among themselves and ordering the official to run the test again. When the results were the same, they made him stand by himself to one side. Not surprisingly, the machine had the same response to Nisha, and she was sent to join Anand.

What would happen to them now? Anand wondered. Would they be able to make the employers believe that they were from the Outer Lands, whatever those were? Would this increase their chances of employment—and thus perhaps freedom—as B had told them? But what if they were asked to describe their home? Even if they made something up, their accounts would differ. Then surely the officials would realize that they were magicians and imprison them forever in the bowels of Rehabitational 39. He felt an urge to chew his nails but forced himself to remain still. It would not do to give away his nervousness.

Fortunately for him, their potential employers were too busy arguing to ask them any questions. Anand realized they all wanted to hire them.

"You got first pick the last time," one of the men accused another. "It's my turn now."

"I can pay more," the third, most elaborately dressed man told the rehabitational officer.

The woman, who had been quiet until then, spoke. "M-81," she said in a cool, clipped voice to the elaborately dressed man, "you know it's illegal to deviate from the flat fee the rehabitational is supposed to charge for all its inmates. If the council came to hear of your offer, they might not look upon it kindly. And they might wonder if perhaps you had more money than was good for your moral well-being." The man paled visibly and started to apologize, but she silenced him with a wave of her hand. To the officer she said, "You know that I have the highest priority, since I have to replace two sick workers—workers that we'd hired from you, I might add—who were supposed to be helping at the banquet the scientists are holding tonight inside Futuredome."

She was a scientist. And she was going to take whomever she chose inside Futuredome, where the conch was locked up. The blood in Anand's temples pounded so hard that he was afraid everyone in the room would hear it. He kept deathly still, afraid that any response on his part might make the scientist change her mind.

"Sign them to my account," the woman said in a voice that expected immediate obedience. The officer hesitated, glancing at the other clients, who looked furious. But in the end none of them dared challenge the scientist.

"The lease has been recorded. They're yours for two days," the officer said once the formalities had been taken care of. He handed her several gadgets, including a blue tube—to keep them under control, Anand guessed—and said his good-byes with some relief. The woman nodded curtly at him and left the building without bothering to check if her newly hired helpers were behind her. She didn't have to. As Anand discovered when he lagged behind for a moment, the collar stung his neck if he was more than a certain distance from her.

Outside, the woman clapped her hands and the back of a white vehicle swung open. Anand observed the vehicle with some curiosity, wondering how it would move, for it had no wheels. The woman motioned impatiently for them to get inside. Like the bus earlier, this vehicle's walls were also made of glass for easy surveillance. The scientist got in the driver's seat and pressed a few buttons, a motor purred smoothly, and the vehicle lifted off the ground and glided forward. They were free of the rehabitational—at least for two days—and on their way to Futuredome and the conch!

Having visited the Farm, Anand thought he knew what domes were like, but as the scientist's van approached Futuredome, he realized that this one was unique. Unlike the other domes, it had a shiny, highly reflective shell, so no intruders could look in. However, clearly those inside could see out, for hardly had their vehicle approached what appeared to be a solid wall when it sprang open—like jaws, Anand thought—and then snapped shut behind them. They were inside what looked like a large, windowless warehouse. Immediately, a host of heavily armed guards surrounded them. Unlike the guards outside, however, they didn't wear masks. Somehow, the scientists had purified the air inside the dome so that its inhabitants could dispense with those irritating breathing devices. The scientist climbed out and removed her mask, too, throwing it, with apparent relief, into the back of the van. She gestured to Anand and Nisha to do the same, then strode up to the leader of the guards, who gave her a deferential bow, confirming Anand's suspicion that she was an important person.

"Please step this way, Dr. S," he said apologetically. "I'm sorry to put you through all this trouble, but I must follow procedures." The scientist stepped into a rectangular box the size of a small room. Anand guessed it was some kind of scanning device to ensure she wasn't carrying any contraband items into the dome. Once she was cleared, Nisha and he were shoved in. The machine sent a tingly sensation through him, then emitted a series of chirps indicating all was clear. Next, a guard moved them on to a different machine, which scanned their eyes and confirmed their lack of records. Finally, the chief guard passed the papers the scientist carried through a third machine to ensure that they weren't forged.

Watching all this, Anand's heart sank. Even if he were lucky enough to find and rescue the conch, how would he smuggle it out past so many guards? And if he failed to rescue it this time and needed to come back into Futuredome, he would never get past this fortress of machines on his own. He sneaked a look at Nisha; she met his glance, lips pursed in grim determination. He could almost hear her pragmatic, no-nonsense voice. *One thing at a time!* In the past she had helped him get through situations as seemingly impossible as this one—when the sorcerer Surabhanu, transformed into a serpent, had attacked him, or when the evil jinn Ifrit was about to burn down the Nawab's court. The memories heartened him. He would worry later. Right now he needed to keep track of the road Dr. S was taking, so that if necessary he and Nisha could retrace it.

As the white van made its way out of the security station and into Futuredome proper, Anand stared in openmouthed surprise. He was seeing something he had taken for granted every day of his life back in his own world: the sun. For inside Futuredome, the sun shone down cheerfully from a blue sky where a few lazy clouds wafted by. If he had not traveled through a dreary wasteland just a few minutes back, Anand would have believed it to be the real thing. How had the scientists been able to create such an amazing illusion? He felt a grudging respect for them but also a deep disquiet: People with such powerful abilities would be hard to outwit. At the same time, he felt the stirrings of anger. They had wasted their abilities on providing frivolous luxuries for the rich and powerful of Coal—but what about the common people? Talking to B had made him realize how harsh their existence was.

The streets of Futuredome were wide and bone white. They looked brand-new—probably because they were only used by hover cars, thought Anand, glancing at the vehicles that glided around him. There weren't many of these, nor were there any pedestrians on the pristine sidewalks. Perhaps most people were at work. All the drivers they passed seemed to know Dr. S. They touched their foreheads or joined their palms respectfully in greeting, though to Anand their smiles looked forced. Were they afraid of her, or just of scientists in general? She gave the briefest of nods in response—she wasn't one to waste her time on social niceties—and headed for a group of steel-gray towers located at the center of the dome.

They were passing a residential neighborhood consisting of perhaps a hundred cheerful multistoried buildings, each exactly like the next, painted in a design of airy pastels: pinks, greens, the palest mauves. There was something about the colors that made Anand's worries recede. A sense of sleepy well-being filled him. Even the danger that engulfed the conch didn't seem to matter. No doubt things would work out for the best; things always did. Next to him, Nisha, too, looked unusually relaxed. As he stared at her, she gave him a woozy smile.

A warning bell went off in Anand's mind. In the valley, he'd taken lessons in Colorpower. He'd learned how, when colors were arranged in particular combinations, they had specific effects on the mind. The colors of the buildings in Futuredome were arranged in a sequence that would discourage inhabitants from asking questions. Was this a coincidence, or had someone purposely designed them this way so that the people who lived in them would be easy to control? He sneaked a look at Dr. S to see how the colors affected her, but she had slipped on a pair of dark glasses.

She knew.

If the scientists of this world were Masters of the subtle sciences, too—fields of study that earlier had been open only to healers and magicians—they would be that much more dangerous. What weapon could Anand possibly use against them?

☙❧

At the tallest, sternest-looking steel tower, there were more guards, and of course more machines. Dr. S drove through a huge one that scanned her entire vehicle, then maneuvered the van up a spiraled ramp to a parking area. She parked in a prime spot close to the rooftop door, jumped out, and clapped her hands to release the young people from the van. A giant cable snaked up from the flooring and clamped itself to the front of her vehicle, powering it for its next use.

The scientist addressed them for the first time, her tone brusque but not unpleasant. "I'll take you to the waiting room. Wash up and get some rest. There'll be fresh uniforms for you there. In a couple of hours, I'll take you to the event, where someone will explain your duties to you. If you're smart, you'll do a good job. Keep in mind that the scientists don't forget easily—nor are they quick to forgive."

They followed her into a glass box that Anand guessed was an elevator. He had never been in one before. In Kolkata, only the most affluent buildings had had them. In any case, he was sure they were nothing like this one, with a transparent floor that made his head spin when he looked down to what seemed like an unending shaft. Dr. S punched in a code, and the elevator plummeted so rapidly that Anand's stomach gave a huge lurch and he had to clutch Nisha's arm to keep his balance.

The waiting area was on the lowest floor. It consisted of a number of locked rooms. Dr. S stopped outside one of these. Its door was transparent so passersby could look in, though Anand guessed that the people inside could not see out. The room was equipped with bunk beds, a bathroom, and a table for meals. Though spare, compared with the cells at the rehabitational it appeared luxurious. The inmates, gathered around a glowing sphere, were avidly staring at projected holograms.

"As you see, the room is equipped with a Podsphere, which you may watch," the scientist said, sounding friendlier than before. "What's your favorite Pod show? I've turned your collars off for the moment, so you can answer."

When Anand and Nisha remained silent, she added in a kind voice, "Don't be afraid!"

"I'm not afraid," Nisha retorted, stung. "We don't have a favorite show because where we come from, there aren't any Pods."

Anand cringed inwardly; Nisha shouldn't have divulged that information! Instead, she should have pretended to be disoriented, perhaps even a little slow in the head.

Excitement lighted up the scientist's face.

"That's what I'd guessed! You're from the Outer Lands! Come with me—no, no, you don't have to stay down here with the other workers. I want you to tell me all about your home."

A nervous Anand followed Dr. S and Nisha back into the elevator. They were in trouble. When Dr. S questioned them, how would they get their stories to match? She was smart. She was bound to become suspicious. And if she guessed where they really came from, and what they planned to do, it would be disastrous to their quest.

Behind the scientist's back he glared at Nisha. *Now look what you've done!* his eyes said. But when he saw how contrite she looked, biting her lower lip to keep herself from crying, he could not bear to stay angry with her.

Sitting on a soft, silken couch, Anand looked around with amazement. The scientist's apartment—for that's where she had brought them—was spare and uncluttered, but the few pieces of furniture with their clean lines showed her fine taste. The open window invited in a cool breeze, and though Anand knew that no natural wind currents could exist inside the dome, he still enjoyed the freshness on his skin. He particularly liked the plant with small purple buds that sat on the windowsill. He had not seen any flowers since he arrived in Shadowland

and had wondered if they existed in this world.

"You like my plant?" Dr. S said, carrying in a platter of bread and fruit and a jug of juice. "We no longer grow flowers in Coal because we need to use all the space we have for food. But I came across these old seeds and thought I would try it at home. I'm waiting for it to bloom. My colleagues think I'm crazy for doing such things! Anyway, here's some food. Help yourselves."

In spite of his nervousness, Anand was too hungry to hesitate. The bread was tasty enough, though unlike anything he'd eaten, and he didn't recognize the juice, though it was very sweet. The scientists, it seemed, had come up with many hybrid foods. He did recognize the bananas, though they were gargantuan and tasted rubbery. But after the mush he had been subjected to at the rehabilitational, he wasn't going to complain! As he took an enormous bite, however, he couldn't help wondering if it had been harvested by an Illegal youth forced to wear a muzzle.

Dr. S leaned back on the couch, put up her feet, and loosened her tightly coiled hair so that soft strands framed her face.

"I shouldn't have brought you to my apartment," she confided. "It's against security procedures. My boss, Dr. X, would be most upset if he knew. But I've been fascinated with the Outer Lands for years. I can't really explain why, except that I have a hunch that there's a wealth of resources hidden there, beyond the Wasted Desert. If we are to save our city, we must find them. So far I haven't been able to convince my colleagues to explore that area. But now, with the evidence I gather from you, I can succeed."

Some of Anand's anxiety must have shown on his face, because Dr. S said, "Don't look so worried! I'm not going to hurt you. I just want you to answer a few questions. What food sources do you have? Do your crops grow in the open, or have you built domes like ours? Do you have to use masks? Where do you get your drinking water? What kinds of power sources do you use? Who are your leaders, and how do they run the community?"

The two friends remained silent. What could they say?

"Why won't you cooperate?" Dr. S said, her voice rising. "Can't you understand the importance of what I'm trying to do? The cities that used to surround us have all collapsed. Coal is the only one left, and it has lasted this long only because we scientists have been working very hard to harvest—uh—other sources of energy. But they're very difficult to come by."

There had been a strange little pause before she said *other sources of energy*. Anand was sure these sources were the objects of power—the ones that the scientists had wrested from the magicians, and the ones that Dr. S's machines had sucked in from other worlds. Anger swept through him as he recalled what had happened to his beloved home as a result of her actions. And yet a part of him could appreciate the difficulty of her task.

"Without energy to create artificial light and clean the air," Dr. S continued passionately, "to purify our water and manufacture our fertilizers so that our farms can grow enough food, Coal, too, would fall apart. We'd all die—but first there would be terrible riots as people fought over the last resources. Is that what you want?"

Anand and Nisha exchanged desperate glances, not knowing what to do. It was crucial that Dr. S not suspect that they came from another world. With her razor-sharp scientist's mind, she wouldn't be satisfied until she discovered how they did it—and how she could make that journey herself. And while she might be reluctant to hurt them to get the information she wanted, Anand sensed that her boss would not mind it at all. Once the scientists found the mirror, how long would it be before they made their way to Anand's world and stripped it of all life?

"I'm waiting!" Dr. S said impatiently. "And don't try to make up something. All of us scientists have been trained in lie detection, so I'd know right away." When they did not respond, her face flushed with anger.

"I can't believe how selfish you are! Even after I explained the direness of our situation and asked for your help, you refuse to cooperate? Or perhaps you're merely stupid. Perhaps you don't realize what can happen to you if you keep up this stubborn silence. Unfortunately, I have to get ready for the party right now. But I promise you, we're going to continue this discussion as soon as we return. And this time maybe I *will* use some of that Hypnoserum Dr. X swears by." She led them downstairs to an empty room, threw some clean uniforms at them, and turned on their silencer collars.

"Just a little precaution so you don't concoct information to lead me on a wild goose chase," she said with a cold smile as she locked them in.

THE PARTY

Balancing a wobbly tray of appetizers in one hand and a stack of napkins in the other, Anand made his way gingerly through the hall. For the moment, he had given up trying to locate Nisha. Presumably, she, too, was weaving through the throng of guests whose elaborately bedecked bodysuits proclaimed their importance.

Anand leaned against the wall for a moment, his arm aching from the heavy tray, and looked around. He was in a large, high-ceilinged hall. Along its shiny walls were positioned numerous Pods like the one he had seen in the waiting room of Dr. S's building. They threw enormous holograms up against the ceiling, each featuring the same face. It was a handsome, intelligent face, with an aquiline nose and a high forehead. In some holograms, it was speaking passionately. In others it offered a sympathetic smile. In others it listened with careful attention. There was something mesmerizing about the face and the colors that swirled around it. Even though a part of his mind recognized the use of Colorpower, Anand couldn't stop himself from falling under the spell of the face. How noble it looked, how kind! To whom did it belong? Would he be here tonight? Would Anand get a chance to approach him and maybe offer him an appetizer? He could not drag his eyes away from the holograms. He wanted to be the one to whom the man listened. He wished he could hear what the man was saying, but his ear shields allowed no sounds to reach him.

Guards had clapped these shields onto each of the Illegals when they arrived at the party. The shields were large and clunky, covering the entire ear. They were designed, Anand guessed, to prevent the servers from overhearing the guests' conversations—for surely at a party filled with the top echelon of Coal, many secret matters would be discussed. He waited with some trepidation to be fitted with a muzzle as well, but to his surprise, there wasn't one. Was this because the guards were certain that no servers at a party this important would dare steal food meant for the guests? Or was it that the Illegals knew how extreme the punishment for such an act would be?

Dr. S had not spoken to Anand and Nisha on their way to the party. She looked striking in a silky white bodysuit with little pearls embroidered onto it, and she had put on makeup that made her lips and eyelids sparkle. But her face had been dark with anger. Illogically—for why should he care what she thought of him?—her disapproval had depressed Anand. In heavy silence she had handed them over to the guards and disappeared among the guests. Watching her stiff back recede, Anand had sighed. For a little while, in her apartment, he had felt they might be friends. But of course that was impossible. His loyalty lay with the conch—the conch, which she had snatched from its home, he reminded himself. Why, then, could he not forget her passionate face as she asked them for help?

The hermit warned us not to get involved in the affairs of Coal, he reminded himself. *Our task is only to retrieve the conch and return to the valley before it's too late.*

There were several appetizers on Anand's tray: a flat bread piled with crisp, baked potato slices, vegetables dipped in batter and fried, and pieces of roasted—was it chicken? No, the pieces looked too large. Anand suspected that it was some kind of hybridized bird. In any case, it was a great favorite. Guests—many of whom had had too much to drink—kept grabbing handfuls from his tray. Anand's stomach growled resentfully as he watched them stuff the appetizers into their mouths and then double over with laughter at a joke. They did not even glance at him, far less spare him a nod of thanks. How different this place was from the Silver Valley, where the lowliest apprentice had been valued, and where the most important healers routinely shared in the humblest chores.

If anything, Anand thought, this place reminded him of the Kolkata he had grown up in, where lavish parties were held for the rich in banquet halls strung with glittery lights, while in the shadows outside, beggars waited for the food that would be thrown into dustbins at the end of the evening. Except here in Shadowland it was worse because the poor could not even get near Futuredome's dustbins.

When his tray was empty, Anand made his way to the back of the room to get another, but the bearded old man swathed in a cook's apron who was refilling trays—another Illegal, judging by his collar—gestured at him to wait. He pointed to the stage at the end of the hall where until now musicians had been performing, indicating that something important was about to happen. Anand stood to the side as he was told. Then something made him glance at the cook again. He drew his breath in sharply, because from this angle the man looked uncannily like Abhaydatta, down to the way he cocked his head intently as he appraised the situation around him. Trembling with excitement, Anand rushed over, the first real smile since he entered Shadowland taking over his face. But the man, though he smiled back, looked perplexed. Clearly, he had no idea who Anand was. Looking closer, an embarrassed Anand could see now that this wasn't his mentor. Longing and loneliness had warped his vision.

The musicians were stepping down, bowing as they passed a hefty man dressed in a suit so white that it dazzled the eye. The man climbed onto the stage, accompanied by a prolonged clapping that hinted at his importance. The more boisterous guests threw their scarves and headgear into the air and cheered to welcome him. As he turned, Anand recognized him. It was the man in the holograms, though in real life he was heavier, and—if his grizzled sideburns were any indication—several years older as well. But in spite of that, he exuded such a powerful magnetism that Anand could feel it even from the back of the hall.

Anand had a hunch that what the man was about to say was crucial to their mission. He longed to hear him, but the ear shields blocked all sound, and from this distance he couldn't read the man's lips. He tried to pull the shields off, but they were clamped on tight. He silently mouthed a spell to enlist the help of a wind spirit to bring him the voice of the speaker, as he had done when he was battling the jinn in the Nawab's court. But the spell failed because all winds had been banished from Futuredome.

He felt a touch on his shoulder. It was the cook, beckoning him to a corner hidden by a curtain. There he reached into an apron pocket and slipped Anand something wrapped in a napkin. Anand opened the napkin to find two small, square golden sweetmeats.

Anand's eyes smarted at this unexpected kindness. Bowing in gratitude, he crammed one of the sweets into his mouth. The other he saved for Nisha, although he knew that if the guards found it on him, he would get into trouble. The sweet—what was it made of? Milk-cheese? Lentils fried with sugar? Here in Shadowland even things that had once been everyday knowledge to Anand grew murky. It tasted different from anything he had eaten, though it was every bit as delicious as he had imagined. He chewed slowly, willing the granules to remain in his mouth as long as possible, but all too soon they melted into his tongue like the energy particles Mihirdatta had described in his class on Transformation. The memory was painful, but along with sorrow, an idea flashed in Anand's brain.

He would try to rearrange the energy particles on his ear shields to create perforations in them. Then he would be able to hear the man.

Anand pulled at the cook's sleeve, gesturing to ask for permission to stay behind the curtain for a moment. When the man nodded, he sank to the ground and closed his eyes to concentrate. Could he do it? He had no more than a few seconds. He had attended only one class on Transformation, and neither of his two previous attempts to practice it had been successful. If there were Blocking Towers nearby, his efforts would be painfully aborted, and whoever monitored the Blockers might trace the disturbance to him. But no matter how high the risk, he had to try. It was his only hope.

He focused his mind on what Mihirdatta had said about everything in the world being formed out of the same energy and tried to become aware of that vast and endless dance of sparks. He visualized his ear shields, hard and black, clipping his earlobes painfully. Then he tried to feel the whirling particles of energy at their core. This, Mihirdatta had said, was the trickiest part—unless he "went" to the level of that energy and became one with it, he could not rearrange it. This is where he had failed before.

If only I had the conch with me, he thought.

He realized, suddenly, that his ear shields were getting warmer. Were they softening, too? He visualized them as pinpricks of shifting light, with tiny holes in the shining design they made. He held his mind there, on the holes, until the dance was all around him, until he was lost in the beauty of the flashing sparks. Until he almost forgot why he had gone there.

"Ladies and gentlemen," he heard a disembodied voice announce, "to top off this delightful, delicious evening, we present to you a man who needs no introduction: the Honorable Dr. X-1, Chief of Scientific Affairs and Leader of the Security Council, and creator of the X-Converter. He will tell you more about the cause for this celebration."

A roar of approval filled the room.

Anand's eyes flew open. He was hearing what was happening in the hall! He resisted the urge to touch his ear shields, carefully masked his elation, and hurried to join a group of waiting servers. Out of the corner of his eye, he noticed the cook give him a knowing stare. Anand's heart thudded in fear. Did the man suspect what had happened? Would he challenge him, perhaps even turn him in? But the man gave a strange half smile and turned back to the trays.

Onstage, Dr. X bowed elegantly, sparking off more applause. So this was Dr. S's boss, the one who swore by Hypnoserum. When he spoke, his deep, attractive voice boomed out over the audience. "Esteemed scientists and councilors, you know that for many years now we have been experimenting with finding alternate energy sources to solve our city's problems. You know, too, that we discovered that magical objects hold a large amount of energy in them— energy that our converters could pass on to the machines that keep us alive. But our problem was that we had few such objects in our world—and what we had was in the hands of the magicians, who insisted on hoarding them in spite of our great need."

Cries of anger rose from the crowd at the reminder of such selfishness.

"With much effort, we retrieved these objects, which the magicians had hidden, by combing Coal with our Finder machines. We ventured even into the depths of the slums, losing many of our brave protectors when the magicians attacked us." Here Dr. X bowed to the armed guards that lined the walls, and they responded with resounding cheers.

"But these objects," Dr. X continued, "were insuf- ficient. We used them up within a few months. Meanwhile, however, through diligent experimentation, we discovered something very exciting. Our strongest machine, the X-Converter"—here he paused modestly for the clapping that swept the room—"was able to sense objects of power from other worlds. At first, it could only pinpoint the places where these objects existed, but recently, after some modifi- cations made by my team, headed by the talented Dr. S"— more cheers—"it actually brought back one of these items.

This object—hoarded, no doubt, by the magicians of that time—was powerful beyond the gauging capacity of our measurer machines!"

The words made Anand dizzy; he had to hold on to the wall. Dr. X was speaking of the conch. Had he already harmed it?

Dr. X continued, "I know I need not emphasize the importance of this event—because, though we've kept the truth from the general population, you who are the leaders of Coal know that in a month we would have run out of the power supply that keeps us alive. But this object, once harvested, can keep our domes functioning for several years!"

Shouts of delight filled the hall. Men and women clapped and danced and hugged each other. Some bowed their heads as though in prayer. If Anand had not been so distraught, he might have sympathized with their relief. But all he could think of was the devastation they had caused in the Silver Valley, and the terrible destruction they were planning.

At least the conch was still safe. That was something to be thankful for.

"We haven't been able to harvest the object as yet because, as you know, a crucial part of the X-Converter was destroyed by the rebel magicians who broke into our laboratory. Dr. S—who incidentally will soon be promoted for her leadership role—has been working most diligently to repair it. She has just informed me that it will be fixed by tomorrow night. The day after tomorrow, then, we will begin conversion.

"I truly believe we have discovered a long-term solution to our problem, for once this operation is successful, the X-Converter can cull more magical objects from other worlds. Since you are the cream of Coal's citizenry and major supporters of the scientists, I wanted you to be the first to know."

This time, the applause continued for several minutes. When it finally died down, a thoughtful, almost secretive expression came over Dr. X's face. He pulled at his earlobe as though he were searching for the right words. "Now that we have enough energy, we can turn our attention to a project dear to all our hearts." His voice deepened further, vibrating inside Anand's head in a familiar manner—as though he were using Persuasion. But how could he possibly know that magical skill?

"It is time," Dr. X continued, "to raze the slums of Coal and get rid of the vermin—the beggars and thugs and especially the magicians—that have been hiding there."

There was a moment of surprised silence as though the crowd was not as enthusiastic about this project as Dr. X claimed. But he did not allow them to think about it for too long.

"Let's drink to a safer and better Coal!" he cried in that same deep, vibrating tone. He made a sign, and a server ran up to him with a tall, fluted wineglass on a tray. He raised it high. The scientists in the front of the hall—his staunchest supporters, Anand assumed—clapped loudly and raised their glasses. The applause was picked up by the rest of the room as Dr. X drained his glass in one suave motion, climbed down, and was mobbed by admirers. Everyone was talking at once, their excited voices filling the hall. Servers were handed trays filled with more celebratory drinks. The music started up again, catchy tunes that made several people take to the dance floor. Anand wove his way through the hall with difficulty, afraid that the jubilant, gyrating crowd would knock his drinks over. At one point he found himself in a corner where Dr. S was being congratulated by her friends. But though she responded with the right words, she didn't look as elated as Anand would have expected.

"I agree—it's a breakthrough."

"Yes, the new energy sources will be very helpful for us."

"Indeed, I'm delighted by the promotion."

After a while, the group drifted away, all except for one haughty-faced woman who said to Dr. S, "So, you've outsmarted me and become Dr. X's favorite of the moment, his golden girl! Well, enjoy it while you can."

Dr. S looked tired. "I'm not competing with you, A. I've told you that ever since we were in school, I just want to do a good job and make things better for our city."

"Right! Next you'll say you didn't even want the promotion."

"I didn't. I would have been happier if instead Dr. X had

given me permission to explore the Outer Lands, as I've been asking him to for years."

"You and your obsession with the Outer Lands! Well, there's no need to go there now. We've solved our energy crisis."

Dr. S looked unhappy. "I don't feel good about scavenging other worlds. Who knows what problems we're causing by removing their objects of power?"

"Grow up, S!" Dr. A said, annoyed. "I don't know what Dr. X sees in you. You always were too queasy to make a good scientist."

"At times," Dr. S continued, as though she didn't hear Dr. A, "I even regret that we learned how to transport these objects through the space barrier."

Dr. A drew in a shocked breath. "Have you forgotten the vow we took when we were inducted? Our first and only duty is toward Coal. What you just said is treachery."

"Why don't you run to Dr. X and tell him?" Dr. S retorted. "Maybe that'll reinstate you as his favorite protégé!"

"I will tell him, one of these days," Dr. A cried. "Then you'll know what regret really feels like."

The two scientists glared at each other; then each stalked off in a different direction.

Anand backed away quickly, not wanting to catch Dr. S's eye. But for the rest of the evening, while he ran up and down, serving and cleaning up, he pondered over the unexpected facets he had discovered to Dr. S's personality: her stormy rivalry with Dr. A and her ambivalent feelings about having brought the conch to Coal.

As he lined up with the other Illegals near the back door, Anand was worried because he had had no chance to transform the perforated ear shields back to their original state. But the guards were busy matching the servers with the scientists who had brought them. They released the controls that had held the shields clamped to the Illegals' ears and instructed them to throw them into a large box. Anand got rid of his shields quickly; then he joined up with Nisha. She looked as exhausted as he felt, and there was a large stain on her uniform where a careless guest must have spilled a drink. At the exit, guards were scanning the Illegals with rods. A few paces ahead of them, a guard pulled a boy out of line and yelled at him to empty out his pockets. Anand's mouth went dry as he remembered the sweet that he was saving for Nisha. But luckily, right then Dr. S drove up. She pointed at them and said something impatiently, and a guard pushed Anand and Nisha into the back of the van.

Dr. S looked tired, as though the evening—and her confrontation with Dr. A—had taken its toll on her. Anand hoped that this meant she would postpone the interrogation with which she had threatened them. But the grim expression that appeared on her face when he met her eye made him realize there was no chance of that. When she had turned her attention to driving, he slipped the sweet he had saved out of his pocket and passed it surreptitiously to Nisha. The pleased surprise on her face made the risk he had taken worthwhile.

They drove in silence. Dr. S was a strange one, Anand thought as he watched the scientist's rigid back. He wondered what he should say when she pressed him with further questions about where he came from.

Tell her the truth. Ask her to help.

The familiar voice inside his head made him jump.

Conch? he asked, astonished. *Are you sure?*

But there was no further word from the conch. Was it annoyed because Anand had doubted it, or was it confined in a place that made communication difficult? He tried to catch Nisha's eye. Maybe she would be able to sense his dilemma and indicate what he should do. But she was dozing.

That must be what it was: his mind, which was just as sleepy as hers, had played a trick on him.

He decided to say nothing to Dr. S. It was too risky. He would focus, instead, on devising an escape plan.

The opportunity Anand was hoping for arrived sooner than expected. Instead of going directly to her apartment, Dr. S stopped in front of a huge black building, looming like some prehistoric monster in the artificial night of Future-dome, where tonight a slivered moon was hidden behind fake clouds.

"I need to check on the X-Converter," she said. "I'll be back in a minute, so don't try anything funny." She gave them a hard stare. "I'll pick up some Hypnoserum, too, while I'm in there." She stepped up to one of the walls and spoke into a tube. After a moment, the wall parted and several guards surrounded her, scanning her with handheld machines. Then they escorted her in, and the wall closed behind her.

Anand shook Nisha awake and gestured to her to stay alert. Next he closed his eyes and concentrated on the double doors at the back of the van, trying to feel the energy particles that formed their essence so he could separate them. But he was too jumpy, too tense, knowing that at any moment Dr. S would return. Every time he began to visualize the dance of light, he was startled by a sound or an anxious thought, and it would vanish. He concentrated so hard that his body started to tremble, and yet he could not hold on to the dance.

Then he felt Nisha's arm come around his shoulders. Even without opening his eyes he could sense the concern on her face. She might not have realized exactly what he was trying to do, but she knew he needed help. He felt her worried love flow into him, thick and translucent as honey. His heartbeat steadied, and his mind cleared. This time he could see the whirling, shining particles. They were like silver crystals. He pressed against them, gently but insistently. For a moment he thought he had failed—the doors were far more solid than the ear shields. Then he heard Nisha gasp. Opening his eyes, he saw a crack between the two doors. The locking mechanism that had held them together was gone!

They put their shoulders to the doors and pushed. Anand had expected resistance, but to his surprise the doors swung open, sending them tumbling onto the street. He struggled to his feet with difficulty, shocked at how much strength the Transformation had sucked from him. Then his eyes were caught by the ominous monolith that loomed over them. So this was the laboratory where the conch was imprisoned. His breath came fast as he imagined it stuffed into an airless vault. Well, it wouldn't have to suffer that fate much longer! He started walking determinedly toward the building, though his steps were shaky. He would go around to the other side of the laboratory and find another entrance— even a small window would do—and coax it open with Transformation. Then they would slip inside and, guided by the conch, find it. Once they had the conch, all the guards in Shadowland wouldn't be able to stop them from returning to the Silver Valley.

But Nisha grabbed his arm and held him back from the harsh glare of the spotlights that were set into the laboratory's walls.

"You're too tired," she mouthed. "You've got to rest first. If you try anything right now, you'll get caught."

Anand tried to remove his arm from her grasp. "I can't stop," he mouthed back, but she would not let go.

Frustration washed over him. How could he abandon the conch and walk away when he was so close? That would be a terrible betrayal. Why couldn't Nisha understand that? She was always causing trouble. He pushed at her with sudden anger. She lost her balance and fell, her mouth an *O* of hurt surprise that made him wretched with guilt. He forced himself to turn from her, to take one step and then another, until he was halfway around the building. Then he formed a Search arrow and directed it cautiously at the wall, trying to sense where exactly the conch was located.

But even that effort was too much for him. His knees buckled and he dropped to the ground. Much as he wanted to deny it, he knew Nisha had been right. He was too weak to attempt any skills at this time, least of all another Transformation.

His fall must have triggered a monitor somewhere, for one of the spotlights mounted on the wall began to swivel in his direction. He tried to crawl off the path, but he was too exhausted to move fast. In a few moments, the light would find him and no doubt set off an alarm.

Then he felt Nisha's hands on him again. Somehow, she wedged her shoulder under his armpit and lifted him up, swaying under his weight. He was afraid they would both fall and be found, but she managed to pull him off the path before the searchlight reached them. He let her lead him, thankful in spite of the huge headache hammering at his skull.

How long did they travel through the dark? Anand was not sure. The place where they ended up was damp and musty. In the distance, he heard the yowl of sirens. Dr. S must have discovered that they were missing and notified the guards. Nisha was scrabbling frantically to clear debris from a small hollow. He wanted to help, but his arms would not obey him. The sirens were getting closer. She pushed him urgently into the small space she had dug out. There was just enough room for Anand to crawl in sideways. Nisha squeezed behind him, her shoulder pressed against his spine. In spite of the dangers that beset them on all sides, her presence made him feel safe. As he gave in to the wave of sleep that broke over him, he wished he could tell her that.

A WAY OUT

Waking, Anand stared up blankly at a low, pocked roof made of concrete that extended about a foot above his head. There was a roaring, swishing sound all around him. Ahead, a little light filtered through a small opening, so that he knew it was morning. Where was he, and how did he get here? Then his memory returned. He craned his neck to look at Nisha, who lay behind him, still asleep, her body curled like a comma to fit into the tiny corner. Seeing her, he couldn't help smiling in spite of his worries. Gingerly, he crawled to the opening, poked his head out, and looked around. He realized that they were underneath a large roadway, just where it lifted up to form an overpass. The ground was uneven here, and strewn with rocks. Some of these rocks had formed a small pocket where they'd been able to spend the night without getting caught. He marveled that Nisha had managed to find such a good hiding place for them, exhausted as she must have been, and he felt freshly ashamed of his behavior last night.

Anand knew they couldn't afford to spend any more time

in their little haven. Guards were probably scouring the area for them. They would be safer outside Futuredome, but how would they pass the gates? And even if they did succeed, how would they breathe once they got outside the dome?

The thought of all the obstacles that lay ahead of him made Anand feel hot and tired. He wanted nothing more than to crawl back into the cool hollow under the roadway and sink back into sleep. But he could not do that. Only five days were left before the Silver Valley froze into its current state of devastation, and they hadn't yet formulated a plan to rescue the conch. He shook Nisha awake, though he hated to deprive her of her few minutes of peaceful oblivion. Nisha rubbed her eyes and started to say something, then clutched her throat where the forgotten collar stung her.

Angrily, Anand tried to snap the collar by twisting it, but the thin metal was unbelievably strong. He wondered if Transformation would work on it. He wasn't sure he had recovered his strength sufficiently to try the skill again, but he felt a great need to talk to Nisha, to hear her voice. He narrowed his eyes, ignoring the headache that felt as though someone had gripped his head in a vise, and focused on the shiny circle of metal around Nisha's neck. Soon he felt the particles of energy spinning inside it. One part of it felt denser, different. That must be where the controls were. He gave it a small push with his mind and felt the particles separate then bounce back in a different formation. He did the same to his own collar; then voiced a cautious hello. There was no pain!

Nisha stared at him, her eyes full of amazement. "We can talk! What did you do, Anand? Was it the same thing that allowed us to escape from the van yesterday?"

Anand basked for a moment in the admiration from her eyes.

"I used Transformation."

"That's a tough skill to master. Thank the Powers that you've learned how to use it! It's been awful not being able to talk. I felt as though I'd burst from all the thoughts boiling inside me. What a strange and scary place this is! I wish we could go back home." Then her face fell as she remembered they no longer had a home to go to.

Anand knew how she felt, but it was no use dwelling on their loss. Instead, he told her what he had discovered at the party. "Now we know where the conch is," he ended, "but how are we going to get to it?"

He had expected Nisha's face to mirror his frustration, but her eyes were shining. "We'll fetch the mirror. It can get us through any door or wall."

Of course! Anand had been too confused last night to think of it. His heart soared—then plummeted again. "But how will we get out past the guards at the dome gates? And even if we do, how will we survive without masks?"

Nisha unzipped the pockets on the sides of her suit. Grinning triumphantly, she pulled out two masks. "Remember, we'd taken them off and left them in the back of the van when we entered Futuredome? Well, last night after the party, I could tell you were planning something, so I put them in my pocket as soon as we got into the van."

Anand took one, impressed by her quick thinking.

"Now we just have to figure out a way to get out," Nisha said. "Our best bet is to follow one of the raised roadways. That was what Dr. S used to get into Future-dome. Maybe there'll be enough space underneath the roadway for us to keep ourselves hidden until we reach a gate."

But what if they went in the wrong direction, away from the gates? Anand thought. They had so little time—they couldn't afford to make mistakes. They needed to ask someone for directions. But whom could they trust?

The familiar voice of the conch floated into his head, though it was disturbingly faint.

You should have been less pigheaded and listened to me when I told you to trust the scientist woman. Now there's only one solution: Look for the collector.

Collector of what? Anand asked. But there was no further answer.

The two friends crawled out of the hole and blended as best they could into the landscape. It was difficult. Apart from a copse of artificial trees planted in front of a tall building a little ahead of them, there was nothing to hide behind on the wide, bare streets.

They had been on the street for only a few seconds when Nisha grabbed his arm. "Someone's spotted us!" she hissed.

A black-uniformed man had come out of the building and was shaking his fist at them, yelling something. Anand's first impulse was to run, but he forced himself to walk toward the man as calmly as he could. He hoped his nervousness wasn't showing on his face.

"You're three hours late!" the man shouted. "The holding tanks are about to overflow, and then what will I tell the tenants?" He glared at him. "Where is the garbage truck, anyway?"

The man—Anand guessed he was the building superintendent—had mistaken them for garbage handlers. And no wonder, thought Anand ruefully, looking down at his rumpled, stained bodysuit. But he was relieved. At least this meant that they wouldn't be turned in to the guards. He had no idea how to respond to the man's question, but fortunately, because of the collar he wore, the man didn't expect an answer.

"I'm going to call the agency and complain," he said angrily, stalking off.

A moment after he had disappeared into the building, Anand heard a loud rumbling in the background. Turning, he saw a truck rattling around the corner. Unlike the sleek vehicles that were the norm in Futuredome, it was old, with rust streaks running down its metal sides. It looked a little like the trucks that used to carry gasoline in Kolkata.

It turned into the driveway where Anand and Nisha stood, then started making its way to the back of the building. Something was written on its side. Rust obscured the lettering, but Anand finally made out the words *Reliable Garbage Collectors*.

His heart gave a leap. Was this what the conch had wanted them to find?

Gesturing at Nisha to follow, Anand ran after the truck, which halted behind the building. The driver backed his truck up to the wall. Then he climbed down with some difficulty—Anand noticed that he was quite old—and pulled out a thick hose connected to the tank. He peered at the keypad on the wall, blinking his eyes.

Anand's heart beat unevenly as he stared at the man's profile.

"Doesn't he look like Mihirdatta, only older?" he whispered to Nisha, but she looked uncertain.

The man punched a set of numbers onto the keypad, and when a circular window opened up, he plunged in the hose, went back to the truck, and switched on a machine. With a loud, slurping sound, the hose began to suck garbage from the vault and into the tank in the back of the truck. When it had cleaned out the vault, the machine shut itself off. The garbage man fought with the hose as he tried to detach it from the window.

Anand knew he probably should not call attention to himself, but he could not stand there watching the old man, who reminded him so much of his teacher, panting and struggling. He came forward and gave him a hand, neatly rolling up the hose so it fitted in its designated space on the side of the truck. The man looked at him with curiosity and some suspicion. Then he gave a brusque nod of thanks and prepared to haul himself back up into his truck. In a moment, he would be gone.

His heart beating rapidly, Anand went up to the old man.

"Please! We need to get out of Futuredome," he said. "Can you help us?"

The man was clearly startled to hear Anand speak in spite of his collar. He himself, impeded by a similar collar, wasn't able to answer. Instead, he shook his head, scowling, and hoisted himself clumsily onto the truck.

"Wait," Nisha said from behind Anand. From the way her voice rang out he could tell she was using Persuasion. Was it his imagination, or had she grown more accomplished? Perhaps danger pushed people to operate at a level beyond what they had believed they were capable of.

The old man paused.

"Can you fix his collar?" Nisha asked Anand.

Anand was not sure that he had enough strength for it. But when he focused his attention on the old man's collar, he was surprised to feel the energy particles shift almost immediately. Were his skills improving, too?

"Say something," he said.

Disbelief was stamped on the old man's face, but he

cleared his throat cautiously. When that did not hurt, he tried a short word, "Who?" His voice was rusty from disuse, but his eyes glistened when he realized that he was able to speak.

"We've come from a different world," Nisha said.

"A different world?" the man repeated incredulously.

"It's too difficult to explain. But please, help us," Nisha said.

Words began to spill from the old man as though he was making up for years of silence. "You given me back my voice. I take you with me. My assistant sick today, is why I late. I pretend you my helpers. Nobody question us. Dome people never care what collectors do. They don't think we also people like them. All they want is us clean their mess."

Relieved, Anand and Nisha helped the old man siphon garbage from several other buildings, unrolling and dragging the heavy hose back and forth so he didn't have to keep climbing down from the truck.

"Thanks," he said with a grateful sigh when the truck was finally full. "My leg hurting bad. I not able to do all work on my own. I afraid dome people complain and I lose job. If old ones lose job, we sent to Outer Lands." Dread colored his voice as he said the last words.

Anand wanted to know more about the mysterious Outer Lands, but they were approaching a gate. He held his breath, worried that the guards would question the old man about having two assistants, but the garbage man had been right. The guards gave them a cursory, uninterested glance and waved them through. Almost immediately, even through the closed windows of the truck, the air stung their throats. Hurriedly, they pulled on their masks. Nisha looked up at the brown sky and grimaced.

"It was nice to have a sun for a while, even a fake one," she said.

But Anand was too concerned with their next move to pay much attention to their surroundings. Closing his eyes, he visualized the mirror and tried to send it a mental signal. But he must have been within the range of the Blocking Towers, for he felt as though he had hit a wall. The pain made him gasp. Nisha stared at him, biting her lip.

"You can't contact the mirror, can you?" she whispered.

Anand shook his head. He thought hard for a moment; then said to the garbage man, "I need to find something important that I left behind. If I describe the place where I hid it, would you be able to take us there?"

"Could be," said the old man. "Did know Coal streets good, one time. Now no more garbage pickup there."

But when Anand described the dark, trash-filled alley under the raised roadways where the mirror had brought them into Shadowland, he gave a bitter laugh. "All Coal look like that now. Must give me street name."

But neither Anand nor Nisha could provide that information.

"What shall we do now?" Nisha asked.

Panic spiraled inside Anand. Time was wasting away, and

they were farther than ever from the conch. Maybe he should have stayed inside Futuredome and taken his chances.

"Wait," Nisha said, "didn't that boy, B, say something when we were at the Farm? Didn't he mention a place we could go for help?"

Anand rubbed his forehead, trying to think past his headache. "It was something about spirits—ah yes, he said we should look for a House of Spirits."

The old man's brows drew together. "House of Fine Spirits! Very dangerous place. No good for you."

"Why is it dangerous?" Nisha demanded.

"Bad things happen. Murders. Vanishing. People there not normal. Spell casters. Even guards not go there except in big troop."

"The people there are magicians," Anand said. "That's why we need to see them."

"No trust spell casters," the garbage man said stubbornly.

Nisha looked like she wanted to argue with him, but she only said, "We'll take a chance. Can you take us there, please?"

The old man gave a reluctant nod. He was not convinced of their safety, but perhaps he saw their determination. They drove in silence for a while. Then he maneuvered the truck off the raised roadway and into an alley. Although by Anand's calculations it was late afternoon—it was hard to tell in this sunless world—there weren't many people on the street, and those who were there walked fast with their heads down, not meeting anyone's eyes. The few shops had

CHITRA LEKHA BANERJEE DIVAKARUNI

bars on the windows and doors. Their curtains were drawn and most looked as though they were closed, though a few times Anand saw movement behind a curtain. The alley was filled with potholes, making the truck bounce up and down. Just before they came to a halt, they hit an especially large one and the old man rubbed his leg, wincing in pain.

"That one," he said, pointing to a small, squat building at the end of the road with sooty walls that looked as though they had been scorched by a fire. The lopsided signboard that hung from it simply said *Spirits*.

The old man swallowed nervously. "I go now."

Anand thanked him and jumped down from the truck, but Nisha leaned toward the old man impulsively and gave him a hug. Then she passed her hand in the air over his sore leg and whispered a few words from a healing chant.

"Leg was hot," the old man said, his eyes wide, "now pain gone!" He stared at them. "You cast spell?"

Nisha nodded.

The old man shook his head hard, as though he were rearranging some of the ideas in there, and gave a reluctant smile. "Not all spell casters bad!"

Anand wondered what had led the old man to hold such a negative view of magicians. But there was no time for questions. Every moment pushed the conch closer to destruction—and the two of them, too, for without the conch, they would be stuck in Shadowland forever.

The old man groped inside a pocket, pulled out a coin,

and handed it to Nisha. When she tried to refuse, he gave a broken-toothed smile. "Not money," he said. "Garbage men not get money, only vouchers for government shops. This from my grandfather."

The two friends looked carefully at the coin, which was embossed with an intricate lettering that looked strangely familiar.

"This, friendship coin," the old man explained. "If you in trouble, show to garbage man or other worker. He help. Good-bye."

Anand and Nisha waved him good-bye, feeling strangely bereft as his truck disappeared around the corner. Nisha peered at the coin in her palm.

"Doesn't the first letter look like something in Bengali? Could it be the letter *M*, for *maitri*, which means friendship? Do you think this coin could have come from our world?"

Anand's mind was snared in worries about what would happen if no one at the House of Fine Spirits were able to help them, but to please Nisha he took a look at the coin. "No, it's just a looped design," he said after a moment. "Come on, it's getting late. Let's go into the shop and see if someone there can help us find the mirror."

Nisha put the coin away. Together, they walked up the crumbling steps of the House of Fine Spirits, wondering what awaited them inside.

THE MAGICIANS

Inside the House of Fine Spirits, it was so dark that Anand was forced to pause at the entrance to let his eyes adjust to the gloom. Behind them, the door swung shut with an ominous crack, darkening the foyer further. Ahead, there was a room, long and narrow, lit only by smoky tapers placed in alcoves. They made Anand feel as though he had stepped back into an older time. The far end of the room was taken up by a bar, where several figures slouched. Along the walls were seating areas shrouded in shadow, so that Anand could not tell if they were occupied.

As Nisha and he walked toward the bar, Anand had the distinct sensation of descending into a river. An invisible current pushed against him, growing stronger with each step so that soon he was struggling to keep his footing. It was a cold, sad current, bringing up memories of loss and failure—the family he had abandoned, the friends he had let down, the skills he had been unable to master. It made him want to lie down and give up, for surely the task that lay ahead was too difficult for an ordinary boy like him. When he looked down, it seemed there were many others—heroes dressed in the noble attire of bygone times, gold-worked robes and headgear glittering with rubies—lying in the river. He saw them under the surface, their bodies still, their faces so peaceful that he longed to join them. His steps grew slower and then stopped.

Did Nisha sense what he was feeling? Perhaps, because she gripped his shoulder and shook it. "What on earth are you doing?" she whispered urgently.

Anand realized that he was kneeling on the floor—no, it was the riverbed. One of the heroes in the water smiled at him, inviting him silently to give up useless strife and lie down next to him.

But Nisha wouldn't let him be. She pulled at his arm, and when he didn't respond, punched his shoulder. He opened his eyes in annoyance—when had he closed them?—to tell her she was more irritating than a gadfly, and that was when she slapped him hard on the cheek. The slap stung, but it cleared Anand's vision. He dragged himself to an upright position. The force of the current seemed diminished now. He could see the uneven floor under his feet. Nisha was crying, "Sorry, sorry," and cupping his face. He wanted to tell her that he was the one who should be apologizing for always causing her trouble, almost causing their mission to fail. How warm her hands were. They sent a surge of comfort through him, countering the spell of this place. That's what he recognized it to be now: a Barrier spell that the magicians must have devised to prevent enemies from invading their sanctuary.

Now that he had recognized it, the spell affected him less. He could move forward again, though his feet still felt blocky and awkward, as though they belonged to someone else. Ironically, he felt more at home in this place than he had inside Futuredome. It was filled with danger—but danger of a kind that he understood.

From the corner of his eye, he could see that the figures that had been standing at the bar were coming toward them, moving with a strange gliding step. He guessed them to be guardians of this space. Their bodysuits were dark blue and hooded, and they were masked like all the inhabitants of Coal. But their eyes, which Anand could see beneath their hoods, glittered with a strange red light.

Quickly, he began to whisper a protection spell to weave a net around them. But their eyes—strangely mesmerizing—distracted him, making him forget key words. The figures slowed, but they kept advancing.

Anand's heart raced with fear as he tried to recall what he knew of guardian spirits. "Keep your face turned away and keep walking," he told Nisha, trying to speak calmly.

"Who—or what—are they?"

"They're protectors of this place—perhaps human, perhaps not," Anand replied. "They can't harm you unless they catch your eye, so be sure you don't look at them." He himself kept his gaze focused on the bar. A little silver bell sat on the warped wood of the counter. Somehow he knew that if he rang it, he would be safe. But the guardians would try to prevent him from doing that.

One of the figures had reached Anand. It couldn't touch him—the protection spell had achieved that much—but it stood right in front of him, blocking his path. A stench of rot came from whatever was under the hood.

"Speak!" it hissed. "Tell us what you're doing here, spy!"

"Spy! Spy! Spy!" The sibilant whisper went around the room.

Anand wanted to blurt out that he wasn't a spy, that he, too, was a magician. But he knew that responding to the creature would increase its power over him.

"Move around it," he said to Nisha. "No matter what it says, don't reply. It can't touch us." He focused his eyes on the bell and his mind on the protection spell, weaving its unraveled parts again.

Behind him, he heard a slimy voice say, "Yes, my pretty, my delicious one, come closer, come to us!"

"Ignore it!" Anand warned. But Nisha cried out, "Get away from me, you filthy, stinking monster!" Then she screamed. The scream was followed by scuffling sounds. Torn, Anand longed to run back and pull her away from her tormentor. But he did not have the strength to fight all the creatures that flocked around them. His only hope for saving Nisha was the bell. Using all his willpower, he continued ahead. The bell was only a few inches away from him now. He reached out for it.

Nisha gave another scream. "Anand! Help!"

Anand stiffened. Nisha should have known not to call out his true name, the knowledge of which gave enemies power over you. She must have been desperate with fear to have forgotten this basic lesson. Did she think he had abandoned her?

He tried to block out the thoughts that raced around his head and reached again for the bell. But he was too late.

A hand shot out from behind the counter and grabbed his wrist. Hard fingers dug into his arm. A tall, cloaked man with piercing eyes glared at Anand. Where had he materialized from?

"Anand, eh?" the man said, eyes flashing. "Soon we'll know everything else about you, too. But first, we'll show you what we do to spies. Come, guardians!"

An electric shock ran up Anand's arm, making him gasp. He didn't know what kind of spell the man was using. He couldn't think of anything to counter it. Whatever it was made him dizzy. His legs could hardly hold him up. Soon, he knew, he would lose consciousness. He could feel the guardians behind him. Nisha gave a despairing cry that was cut off abruptly.

With the last of his strength, he lifted his left hand and sketched in the air the sign that B had made, long ago, at the Farm. His head was swimming, and he was not sure that he remembered it correctly.

"B told me to come to you," he croaked as he fell, face forward, onto the counter.

☙

Anand was dimly aware of hands. Hands that grasped his arms and legs and were carrying him somewhere. Human hands, thank the Powers! They weren't particularly gentle, but at least they didn't attempt to hurt him. Now they were jostling him—down a flight of stairs, it seemed. He kept his eyes closed because he wanted to learn as much as he could while they thought he was still unconscious.

"Maybe you're right," one of the men carrying him said to the other. "Maybe he *is* a friend of Basant's, like he claimed. But I think Commandant Vijay is correct in being cautious."

Anand was so startled he almost opened his eyes. Basant? Vijay? The magicians had Indian names! Did this mean that at some point when they still possessed the skill to do such things, they had traveled to Shadowland from Anand's world?

"What I want to know is, how on earth did he and the girl get past the River of Dejection?" someone else said. "We thought it was foolproof!"

"That's part of the reason why the commandant is so concerned. If the scientists have discovered a way to get past our strongest conjurations, then we're really in trouble!" a third voice said. Evidently there was a whole contingent of people transporting him.

"I agree with Vijay. He's a spy sent by the scientists," a different voice burst in. "And if he can't satisfy us as to why he's here, he's going to be in deep trouble."

"Yes, we'll give him some of their own medicine!" This time it was a woman's voice, spitting out the words. "When I think of my poor Basant, and all our other boys, stuck in that prison for months now, doing hard labor! Who knows how else they're torturing them—"

"Hush, all of you!" The other man carrying him spoke, his tones deeper and calmer than the others. "That's why we're taking him to Chief Commandant Deepak. He can look into a person's heart and see his truth."

The magicians fell silent. Only one person muttered, somewhere behind Anand's head. "I'm not so sure of that anymore, not since the scientists killed his son—and now with his grandson a prisoner—" The muttering faded away.

ᘯᘯ

A splash of cold water hit Anand's face. He gasped and opened his eyes, blinking as though he had just come to. He found himself in a small room without windows—somewhere underground beneath the House of Fine Spirits, he surmised. The room was crowded with men and women dressed in bodysuits. Unlike the pristine white suits the scientists wore, the magicians' clothes were a motley of colors, often threadbare. One looked like a garbage collector's outfit; another was similar to what the cook had worn at the party. Anand guessed that the magicians had been forced to take up different jobs in order to survive after they went into hiding. Perhaps these disguises also helped them gather news.

Then he noticed that none of them wore breathing masks. His mask, too, had been removed. The air in the room, though dank and stale, did not burn his lungs. In spite of the danger facing him, Anand was intrigued. Somehow the magicians had learned to clean the air of Coal sufficiently to make it breathable.

In front of him, in a big carved-wood chair, sat a stooped old man dressed in a blue robe. This had to be Basant's grandfather, Chief Commandant Deepak, the leader of the magicians. Anand examined him carefully. His long gray hair fell to his shoulders and a white beard covered most of his chest. His eyes were sunken, as though he had not slept well for many nights. Still, they were deep and wise and looked at Anand as though they could indeed see into his soul. Anand knew that he should be cautious—maybe even frightened—of this powerful man, but somehow he was not. The old man's eyes reminded him of Somdatta, the Chief Healer of the Silver Valley, who had always been fair, and he had the same aura of calmness.

Impulsively—for he was not usually demonstrative—Anand raised his hands—realizing only now that they were tied together—and joined them in greeting.

"Greetings, Master Deepak Datta," he said, bowing as he would have to one of his teachers.

A murmur of surprise rippled through the room. The old man raised his eyebrows. "That is the way our forefathers were addressed, many generations ago. How do you know this? And how did you get past the obstacle that protects our lair, we who have been reduced to living like wild beasts? Who are you, stranger?"

Quickly, Anand explained their mission. Around him, the room grew still as people listened with rapt attention to his story. "Please release Nisha," he pleaded, "and help me find the Mirror of Fire and Dreaming. Once I have it, I can rescue the conch, which is very wise and powerful. I am sure it can tell us the best way to rescue Basant and the other imprisoned magicians."

Chief Deepak said, "You speak of unbelievable things. I should suspect you, like my nephew Vijay does, but somehow you have gained my trust. Your amazing accomplishments—traveling from another realm, escaping from Futuredome, and finding us—give me confidence that you will succeed in your quest. But even otherwise, we would have helped you, for being magicians—no matter from which world—you are kin to us." He gestured to an attendant. "Release this boy's companion and bring me the Watchful Bowl. And oh yes—untie his hands."

A deep voice resounded from the back of the room. "With all due respect, Uncle, I don't think you should untie the boy or his friend. Who knows what powers they are hiding? Even if they are magicians, how can we be certain that they haven't defected to the side of the scientists? Others have done it before."

As he spoke, the man strode forward, his royal blue cloak streaming behind him. It was the man who had grasped Anand's wrist earlier! The crowd parted deferentially, and Anand could see that the younger men paid more attention to him than they had to the chief. He came to a stop in front of Anand, scowling at him. "In fact, I suggest that we add a magical binding to their ropes," he said.

"No, Vijay." The chief spoke softly, but in a resolute tone. "A scent of goodness rises from this boy. He and his companion are our guests now."

The stiffness with which the commandant held himself indicated that he didn't agree, but out of respect he said no more.

Four men entered, carrying a heavy stone slab with a hollow in its center, and set it in front of Chief Deepak. Two others escorted Nisha in. Her hair was askew and her sleeve was torn, but she looked more defiant than afraid. When she saw Anand, she ran over to join him.

"Are you all right? Did they hurt you?" she asked, linking her arm through his and throwing the commandant a smoldering glance.

A woman, her face bearing a striking resemblance to

Basant's, brought water in a pitcher and poured it carefully into the hollow.

"Vijay," the old man said. "You must join me in the Seeing. You know that I am no longer strong enough to do it myself."

The commandant couldn't ignore this invitation. He joined them, placing his hands over the stone so that his fingertips touched the water, but his haughty face with its handsome, high cheekbones exuded displeasure. The chief followed suit and gestured to Anand to do the same. Once all three of them were touching the water, he asked Anand to close his eyes and visualize, as clearly as he could, the place where he had left the mirror.

Anand did as he was told, trying to remember every detail: the heaps of garbage on the corner; the graffiti on the abandoned warehouses; the angle of the skyway overhead. Somewhere in the background, he heard a woman's voice chanting. Was it Basant's mother? He hoped there would be an opportunity for him to speak to her, to tell her how helpful and kind her son had been. He could feel the mental energies of the other two magicians swirling around his thoughts, trying to decode them.

"I think I recognize the building," he heard Chief Deepak say. "Isn't that the old warehouse in the Sixth District where they used to store refrigerators—when we had enough electricity for common people to use such things?"

Vijay said, "I'm not quite sure. I need a few more minutes."

Anand concentrated on the images again, but this time he had a strange feeling, as though someone was probing his mind, no longer trying to examine the scene he was recreating, but going below it to search his other thoughts. It made him uneasy and fidgety, and after a moment he opened his eyes.

"I tell you, it's the refrigerator warehouse," the chief was saying to Vijay. "I saw the broken signboard for the Terrace Flats, which are right next to it. You must have seen that, too!"

Vijay seemed distracted, and his uncle had to repeat his statement.

"Yes, I saw it this time," he finally responded.

Anand had a feeling that Vijay had been certain of the place from the very first but had wanted to pry into Anand's mind. He did not like what the commandant had done. But could he really blame Vijay for wanting to make sure Anand was not a threat to his people?

"I'll take the boy there and try to find the mirror he speaks of," Vijay was saying. "But our chances of recovering it are slim. With the Finder machines scanning the city constantly, the scientists have probably captured it already."

Ice gripped Anand's chest as he heard Vijay's words. The mirror might be able to hide itself from human eyes, but what about machines that were specifically designed to detect magical energy?

Vijay's wrong, he told himself vehemently. *He doesn't know objects of power like I do.*

But his heart was heavy, and looking at Nisha, he could see that she, too, shared his misgivings. Even though they were hungry, they refused the chief's invitation to eat with the magicians and set off.

∽~∾

Anand surmised that it was evening by the time he and Nisha stepped out of the old van, stretching their cramped limbs. Had four days passed already? Time was getting blurry in his mind. Vijay had made them sit in the back, squeezed next to boxes filled with tools. Anand gathered that he made his daily living as a handyman, working with the poorer inhabitants of Coal so that he wouldn't attract the attention of the scientists. It made Anand sad to think that the proud magician had been reduced to this.

Vijay had not wanted to bring Nisha along. He said that too many people wandering around the Sixth District, which was supposed to be abandoned, would make the guards suspicious. Anand didn't like the thought of leaving Nisha behind, but he could see that Vijay had a valid point. He remembered how quickly the police had found them when they first appeared in Shadowland. He would have given in, but Nisha refused to be left behind. She made such a fuss that the chief said to Vijay, "Oh, take her along!"

Vijay could not go against the chief's words, but his thin nostrils flared with anger and he gave Nisha a dark look.

Now Vijay climbed down from the front of the van, along with another magician whom he had brought along.

"Hurry!" he said to Anand. "Patrols are sent to the abandoned areas every hour, and we don't know when they were here last. Do you recognize the place?"

Anand nodded. There was the torn mattress, just as he'd left it. He ran toward it, calling silently to the mirror. To his great relief, he felt an answering throb of energy. He rummaged among heaps of stuffing and felt its sharp edge against his fingers.

I'm so thankful I found you! he said. *I need your help!*

I'm happy, too, and ready to do what you need. The reply formed inside his head. *I sense danger, though—*

Anand swiveled around, but the skyway above Nisha and the magicians was empty.

"Is this the mirror you spoke of?" Vijay asked, eagerness brightening his deep-set eyes. "And can it truly take you anywhere you wish to go?"

Anand nodded.

"May I take a look? I've never seen such a powerful magical artifact before." Vijay put out his hand. To Anand's surprise, he noticed that the commandant's fingers were trembling. He felt a surge of sympathy. How hard it must be to be a magician in this world, bereft of the support of objects of power! He thought of how dismal his own life would have been without his friendship with the conch. But as he began to hand it over, a strange thing happened. The mirror grew heavy, as though it didn't want to go to Vijay.

Wondering what this meant, Anand pulled it back and held it to his chest.

"What's the matter?" the commandant asked, annoyed.

"Let's get away from this place first. You yourself said it was dangerous. Once we're back at the House of Fine Spirits, I'll show it to both you and the chief. He can tell us how best to get back into Futuredome and rescue the conch."

"I can tell you that," Vijay said impatiently. "In fact— even better—I'll take you there myself. Just let me see the mirror." He held out his hand.

Something about the magician made Anand uneasy. He backed away into the alley. To his alarm, Vijay followed him and lunged at the mirror. Anand was barely able to dodge away.

"Grab him!" he heard Vijay yell to his companion, who ran at Anand. To his shock, Anand realized that Vijay desired the mirror for himself. Was that why he had not wanted Nisha along, so there wouldn't be any witnesses? He wanted to use it to enter Futuredome with guerrilla troops—the young men who hung on his words—and wreak further havoc on the scientists and their machines. Instinctively, Anand felt that such an action would only worsen the situation in which the magicians found themselves. Moreover, it would ruin his plans for rescuing the conch—and he could not allow that.

Desperately, he dodged low, feeling hands brush his hair.

Nisha had realized what was going on. She grabbed random objects from the garbage pile—a broken pot; a mangled shoe; a thick book, its pages damp and swollen—and threw them at the men. A chair leg struck Vijay on the shoulder and he yelled in fury and turned toward Nisha. Anand used that opportunity to slip past him. Then Nisha and he were sprinting as fast as they could, turning into one alley and then another in an effort to evade their pursuers. Soon they were hopelessly lost and out of breath, but they hadn't managed to shake off the magicians, whose curses they heard close behind. Anand tried to set up a protection barrier, but the Blocking Towers sent a spear of pain through him. Fortunately, the towers prevented the magicians, too, from using spells.

Somewhere nearby, Anand heard the cough of a truck's engine. Were more magicians coming to Vijay's assistance?

"It's around this corner," Nisha panted, pointing. "Maybe it's our friend the garbage man." Before Anand could caution her, she ran toward the sound. Following her, he saw that it was not the garbage truck they had been on but a smaller vehicle.

Nisha placed herself directly in front of it. With one hand she searched the pockets of the bodysuit while with the other she waved at it to stop.

The truck did not even slow down.

The magicians had turned the corner. They were only about twenty arm's lengths behind them, gesturing furiously.

"Thief! Thief!"

Anand knew they needed to run. Clearly the truck would not stop—especially now that the driver saw the men pursuing them. It was too dangerous in Coal to get involved in other people's business. Anand tried to drag Nisha off the road, but she stubbornly held her ground. She had found what she had been searching for, the coin the old garbage collector had given them. She waved it at the driver.

Anand was sure the driver wouldn't be able to see the tiny coin. He yanked at her arm, but she pushed him off with unexpected strength.

"Help us!" she yelled, using Persuasion. The next moment she doubled over in pain.

There was a horrible shrieking of brakes. The truck came to a shuddering stop just a few hand spans from them. The driver, a young man with sweaty streaks of dirt running down his face, threw open the door on the passenger side. Did he look like Raj-bhanu, the young healer who had brought Anand the message from Abhaydatta that had begun this whole nightmarish adventure? There was no time to check. Nisha clambered in and Anand followed, slamming the door behind him. He locked it and tried to put up the window, but it got stuck halfway. Remembering his earlier experience, he aimed his mind at the collar around the young man's neck and held it there in spite of pain until he felt the particles shift.

"You can speak now," he told him.

The driver looked stunned at all that had happened. "Don't know why I stopped. Nothing but trouble in it."

Nisha showed him the coin. "Please, go as fast as you can. We've got to get away from those men. We're not thieves! They're the ones trying to steal what we have. You have to believe me!"

The young man took the coin, bit it, slipped it into his pocket, and pressed down on the accelerator. "Thief or not, doesn't matter to me. You got a friendship coin. Favor for favor—that's the workmen's motto. But this truck, she can't go too fast—"

There was a loud thunk on the side of the truck. Vijay had jumped onto the footboard and was hanging on to the window as he reached inside with his other hand, trying to grab the mirror. Anand tried to push him off, but he was too strong—and too determined. He lunged again and almost got the mirror this time. The driver swerved, trying to throw the commandant off. But Vijay hung on, grim-faced, while Anand found himself sliding helplessly toward the window. Vijay didn't miss this opportunity. He grasped the mirror. Anand hung on to it with both hands, but Vijay was more powerful. In a moment, Anand knew, Vijay would wrest it from him.

"Help!" he cried, not sure whom he was entreating.

"Doing the best I can," the driver yelled, speeding up until the truck shook. Nisha beat at Vijay's iron grip, but it didn't loosen. Instead, Anand's sweaty palms began to slip. Vijay laughed, his teeth sharp as a tiger's.

Just then a dazzling ray of light burst from the mirror right into Vijay's eyes. He gave a shout, let go of the mirror, and clapped a hand to his face. The driver saw his chance and swerved again. This time it worked. Vijay fell from the truck onto a pile of garbage. He sprang up at once, but it was too late. Anand felt his furious glare following them as the truck turned a corner.

Anand held the mirror close to his chest with one arm and put the other around Nisha. He could feel her shaking.

"I didn't trust him," she said. "But I never thought he'd try to take the mirror from us by force."

"I guess he was desperate," Anand said.

The driver shot a wary glance at them.

"Don't want to get caught in fights between spell casters," he said. "I'm going to drop you off right here." He brought the truck to a screaming halt.

"Please," Anand entreated, "we need to enter Futuredome. Just get us past the gates. We can pretend we're your assistants."

The young man snorted with laughter. "You got a hope! We don't even have the same uniforms. And guards screen all trucks going in with a Finder machine. They'll find that thing you're holding right away. Just get off here." He reached across them and flung the door open.

Anand's heart fell. But Nisha put a hand on the driver's arm while she touched the mirror with the other. Anand thought he saw a shimmery light leap from the mirror into her chest.

"Listen to me," she said, her voice at once so firm and sweet that even though she wasn't speaking to him, Anand immediately wanted to do whatever she suggested. "If we succeed, it will save more people than you can imagine—not only in my world, but here. My hope is that it will change this Shadowland into a place of light."

If she was using Persuasion, it was stronger and subtler than anything Anand had ever observed in the Silver Valley. But no—it was simpler: She spoke what she truly believed and allowed it to do its work. Had the mirror taught her to do that?

"Will you help us?" Nisha ended.

The driver blinked as though waking from a dream. "I'll drive you up to the side of the dome, to a part that can't be seen from the entrance gates. That's the best I can do."

"That will be enough," Nisha said. Anand was astonished at how certain she sounded. "Beyond that point, the mirror will take us where we need to go."

THE LABORATORY

Anand and Nisha crouched in the corner of a room behind a massive file cabinet. Nisha craned her neck out cautiously, trying to figure out where exactly they were, but Anand sat still, striving to gather his thoughts. He could not believe that they had succeeded in entering the sleek, black monolith that was the stronghold of the scientists without being intercepted by the numerous guards that infested its corridors. If only they could get to the vault now! There was no space for error, for in a few hours the conch was scheduled for destruction. Nor could he forget that, even as he sat here, the universe was hardening itself around the transformed, icy valley that had been his beloved home.

A few minutes ago, the truck had left them on a barren stretch of land outside the back wall of Futuredome. Remembering how he had used the mirror long ago to get into the palace of the Nawab, Anand had held it against the dome's curved surface. Though he knew what would happen, he was amazed once again as the mirror changed, growing pliant and transparent, and then disappearing. In its place was now a hole, large enough for Anand and Nisha to squeeze through.

Once they had entered Futuredome, where fake stars were already twinkling in the fake night sky, the mirror gave Anand further directions. *Imagine the place where you want to go. Now that we are inside the barrier, I can transport you directly there if you give me a clear mental picture.*

Removing his mask, Anand had placed the mirror on the ground. He had pictured the hulking black building he had tried vainly to enter—was it only yesterday? He imagined the inside of it as best he could: snaking corridors leading to areas of secret research and experimentation, filled with sleek, shining machines that hummed ominously. The mirror had begun to glow. Just as he stepped into it, an image came to his mind unbidden. A large stainless-steel desk with Dr. S sitting behind it, bending over a pad with notations on it, her brow furrowed as she worked her way through a problem.

Why on earth had he thought of her?

Now as he peered surreptitiously from the other side of the file cabinet, he knew exactly where the mirror had brought them.

Dr. S's office was disconcertingly white: white walls, white ceiling, dazzling white lights that shone from every corner. There were several stainless-steel file cabinets, as well as a number of machines whose functions Anand could not guess. In the middle of the room was a large desk very much like the one he had imagined, except it was empty.

Naturally. It was night now. Dr. S must be back in her airy, pretty apartment, so different from this sterilized place. Along with relief he felt an inexplicable sense of disappointment because he would not see her again. He wondered if the purple plant in her house had flowered.

Nisha had run over to a small cabinet and opened it. "Food!" she cried, holding up what looked like a bar of chocolate.

Anand's mouth watered. He suddenly realized he was starving. He could not even remember when he had last eaten. Was it at Dr. S's apartment?

There was a sound outside the door. Nisha quickly stuffed a couple of bars into her pocket before they both ran to their hiding place. "We'd better get out of here," she said. "Let's ask the mirror to transport us inside the vault. Then we can get the conch and go home."

She was right. But Anand wanted to take another look around the office, to find something that would tell him a little more about Dr. S. He listened carefully. Outside the office, all seemed quiet. "In just a minute," he said, as he walked over to her desk. There were several neat stacks of paper, but they were written in a code that he couldn't decipher.

Suddenly the door swung open, and Dr. S entered the office with an armload of files. Anand had no time to hide. For a moment she stared at him, eyes wide with incredulous fury. Then, before he could say anything, she ran to her desk and pressed a button—to summon the guards, he guessed.

"You mustn't turn us in!" he whispered. "We've got to

talk. I have something important to show you."

"Why should I trust you?" the scientist hissed. "Do you know how much trouble you landed me in, escaping from my car like that?"

There wasn't time for Anand to say anything in his defense. He heard footsteps running toward the office and ducked behind the cabinet.

The door burst open. "Dr. S!" a voice said. "You activated the intrusion alarm. Did you see or hear something?"

Anand held his breath, waiting for her to point them out, for the guard's heavy hand to descend on his shoulder, for the trip back to Rehabitational 39. Would they find the mirror on him and turn that in to Dr. S, to be harvested along with the conch?

Then he heard the scientist say, "We're conducting a study on how long it takes for our guards to respond to the alarm. You've done excellently, F-1776! I'll be sure to recommend you to your supervisor." She walked out with the guard, talking to him as she went. The door swung shut soundlessly behind them.

Nisha let out a huge sigh of relief. "Whew! I was sure she'd turn us in! If we hurry, the mirror can get us into the vault before she returns."

Anand wavered. Nisha was right. He knew he should do what she suggested. Yet he was reluctant to betray Dr. S's trust again. "Something tells me we should wait for Dr. S— she did protect us from the guards, after all. I'm going to confide in her this time, like the conch advised me to."

"The conch?" Nisha asked in surprise. "Why would it say that?"

"We'll find out."

In a minute, Dr. S returned. She clicked a few buttons, and large metal sheets descended from the ceiling to cover the door and windows of the office.

"No one can interrupt us now," Dr. S said. She looked sternly at Anand. "Start talking. You'd better have a good explanation, otherwise I'm going to press that button again, and this time the guards *will* find you and take you away."

Anand racked his brains. What could he say to convince Dr. S of the rightness of his mission, to stop her from destroying the conch? She probably saw it as *her* mission to do so—the only chance she had to save her city from ruin.

Conch! he implored. *Tell me what to do!*

A thought came into his mind, but it was very weak. Was the conch losing its power in this poisonous environment?

Love.

What could the conch mean by that ambiguous message?

Dr. S drummed her fingers on her desk, looking exasperated.

Anand turned to Nisha to see if she had any ideas. She offered him a worried smile. How sweet her face was, in spite of its tiredness, its grime—and her eyes. He was struck by the fact that he cared for her more than any human he knew. No matter what happened, he was glad she was here to share it with him. He reached for her hand, and suddenly, as her trembling, slightly moist fingers clasped his, he knew what he needed to do.

"I'm going to tell you a story," he said to Dr. S.

The story Anand began was that of his own life as an unhappy boy, forced to work at a roadside tea stall because his family was too poor to afford an education. "Life was rough and full of despair in the slums of Kolkata," he said.

The scientist's eyes widened in surprise. "Did you say Kolkata? Why, that's the name our city was known by several hundred years ago! How could you have lived here then, and if you did, how did you get here now?"

Anand was too shocked to respond. This hellish place (not Coal, he realized, but *Kol*) with its unbreatheable air and sunless sky, its extravagant domes that separated the fortunate few from the desperate masses, was not a different world, as he had assumed all this time. It was what his hometown had become. In spite of his own difficult life, he had several beautiful memories of the city. He had strolled along the banks of the Ganga, enjoying the evening breeze and the twinkle of lights on the Howrah Bridge. He had fed giant carp on weekend mornings at Rabindra Sarobar Lake and watched them play hide-and-seek under the lotus leaves. He had climbed the monument and looked down on rooftop terraces where colorful saris were hung up to dry. A heaviness filled his heart at the fate of the city of his birth. Along with that came a rush of anger. All this time he'd been thinking that the valley had been devastated by strangers from another world. But it was his own people who had done it, reaching back into the past with their destructive, greedy grasp.

"Well," prompted Dr. S, "how did you get here?"

Anand was too upset to answer, but Nisha, who had dealt better with the shock of finding out the identity of Kol, said, "We traveled through time."

Anand stared at her in consternation. She should not have given Dr. S that crucial piece of information. What if the scientist tried to snatch the mirror from them like the commandant had done? What if she called in the guards with their tubeguns to assist her? Anand and Nisha would never be able to escape from them.

Nisha shrugged her shoulders defensively. "You said we should trust her!" she said.

At the comment, Dr. S glanced from Anand's face to Nisha's, an unreadable look in her eyes, and started to say something in response. But, avid scientist that she was, she caught herself and got back to business.

"Did you really travel through time? How did you manage that? We scientists have been trying to create a time machine for ages—because in spite of all our efforts, we're afraid life in our world will soon become unsustainable. Can I see the machine you used?"

"Only after I show you something else," Anand replied.

He went on with his story, describing how he had wished

and prayed for something to change, and how—almost as though in response—Master Abhaydatta had come into his life, asking for his help to return the magic conch to the Silver Valley. He told Dr. S of a few of his adventures along the way, and then described the valley.

His voice trembled as he spoke of how amazingly beautiful it had been the very first time he saw it, enclosed by icy mountains, its beautiful parijat trees laden with fragrant silver blooms. How fortunate he had felt when he walked into the Great Hall, with its hundred pillars and its crystal roof through which the stars shone, and was chosen as one of the Brotherhood. How special it had been to study, with the rest of the apprentices, in the Hall of Seeing and on the Watchtower Tree, communicating with distant parts of the world, ready to help all who were in need. Nisha joined in, telling Dr. S about Mother Amita, the herbmistress, and how she taught Nisha to use plants to cure even the worst illnesses—until the final day, when she and Anand had returned from their journeys to find a frozen wasteland.

"That's what your X-Converter did when it dragged the conch into the future," Anand ended. "I don't know what happened to the rest of the Brotherhood. Some are probably caught in the abyss. But others were pulled into this world with the conch. I've glimpsed them, great magicians now doomed to live out their lives in drab, menial labor."

Uncertainty flickered in Dr. S's eyes. "I had misgivings from the first, but I never thought our machine would do something so terrible," she whispered, half to herself.

"That's why you must help us take the conch back home. It's our only hope of setting things right," Anand said.

But Dr. S had forced a professional expression onto her face. "I'm sorry for what happened to your people," she said in formal tones. "But I can't give the conch back. My people need its energy in order to survive."

"Didn't you understand anything we said?" Nisha cried passionately. "To you the conch is nothing but a big battery, something to keep your domes going so you can keep enjoying your fake sunshine and your hover cars. Well, I have news for you. It is a Being. It's older and more important than all of us. We're not going to let you destroy it! Maybe we should have listened to the commandant and helped him to blow up your entire lab."

Dr. S's face grew dark at the mention of the commandant. "You've been with the magicians, haven't you?" she cried. "Did they send you here to do more damage? Tell me what they're planning, or I'll call the guards!"

Nisha turned to Anand. "You should have listened to me when I told you to go to the vault! But we can still do it. She can't stop us. Once we free the conch, it'll protect itself— and us, too."

Still Anand hesitated. The conch had told him to trust Dr. S, and though right now she didn't look particularly reliable—in fact, she looked as though she was reaching for the security button again—he needed to give it a try.

"You wanted to see the machine that brought us here?" he asked. "If you sit back quietly, without calling the guards, I'll show it to you." He brought out the mirror from behind the file cabinet.

"Why, that's just an old image reflector," the scientist said angrily. "Are you playing games with me?"

Anand cradled the mirror for a moment in his arms, trying to decide what to say to convince her. Either way, it was risky. If she didn't believe him, she would summon the guards to take him away. And if he did convince her, she would probably snatch the mirror from him and put it in the vault to be destroyed along with the conch

To his surprise, words formed inside his mind.

Put me in her hands.

The mirror, which hadn't wanted to be touched by Vijay, who was a magician, was willing to go to Dr. S, the woman responsible for all of the Brotherhood's woes! Anand was perplexed, but he obeyed.

Holding it out to her, he said, "This is the Mirror of Fire and Dreaming, which brought us here."

Dr. S gave him a disbelieving glare, but she took the mirror from his hands. She turned it over and examined it, tapping the back and then the front, checking for hidden controls. Anand stiffened. One of the first lessons he had been taught in the valley was to treat objects of power with the greatest respect. Beside him, Nisha let out her breath in an angry rush. "Take it back from her," she cried to Anand.

But even as Dr. S tinkered with the mirror, a strange look came over her face. Her hands stilled, and her breathing grew slow and regular. Though her eyes were open, it was as if she had fallen asleep.

"The mirror has pulled her into a waking dream!" Nisha whispered.

Anand remembered what Abhaydatta, a Master of the art of remembrance and forgetting, had told him once about waking dreams. Sometimes a person's mind blocked out something important—something without which he or she couldn't function as a whole human being. The blockage usually occurred because of a traumatic event or psychic interference, but unless it was removed, the person couldn't live fully. Usually an experienced healer such as Abhaydatta could put such a person into a waking dream and remove the block—but it seemed that the mirror had the same power.

"That's why it's called the Mirror of Fire and *Dreaming!*" Anand exclaimed.

"Shhh!" Nisha cautioned. "It's showing her something."

Dr. S's lips were moving, though she made no sound. She held the mirror very close, and smiled as if she were looking at someone dear to her. Her face had taken on an intense, listening look. Then her expression grew sorrowful and tears formed in her eyes. A drop splashed onto the mirror.

The teardrop must have broken the trance, for Dr. S looked up. Her eyes were unfocused, and she looked around as though she did not recognize where she was.

"Dr. S," Anand said in concern, "are you all right?"

She gave a start and stared at him as if she'd never seen him before. Anand's heart lurched as he wondered if he'd been mistaken. If instead of making her remember, the mirror had made her forget who she was in order to protect them—and the conch—from her. In spite of all she had done to the Brotherhood, he didn't want that to happen to her.

But then she said, in a clear voice, "Yes, I'm fine." She wrapped the mirror carefully in a padded plastic sheet and placed it inside a pack that she strapped onto her back. She filled a large black bucket with water from a sink in the corner of her office and clamped a lid over it. Then she took out two white bodysuits, complete with masks and bulging safety goggles, and lobbed them at Anand and Nisha. She pulled on a similar mask herself and hit the switch that controlled the metal sheath covering the door. "What are you waiting for?" she said impatiently. "Let's get to the vault."

The vault was a small room, much smaller than Anand had imagined. Its walls were formed of a gleaming black metal that must have had a certain blocking power, for as soon as Anand stepped inside, he felt as though his head was wrapped in a thick, clammy towel. He had expected to see a safe inside, but it was totally empty except for eight guards who stood, two at each corner, with their blue tubeguns ready. They looked surprised to see Dr. S, but did not appear suspicious yet.

Anand glanced at Nisha. He could tell she was thinking the same thing as he was: It was a good thing that they had not attempted to enter the vault on their own.

In her most clipped, businesslike voice, Dr. S informed them that her Analyzer machine had just alerted her to the fact that the object inside the vault had reached a volatile state and might explode at any moment. In fact, they were lucky that it had not done so already. She needed to place it immediately in a container of XB Neutralizer (here, Nisha, who was carrying the bucket, sloshed it loudly) and remove it from the premises. They were welcome to watch while she and her assistants performed this dangerous task, but frankly, she did not advise it.

The guard in charge nervously informed her that they would rather wait elsewhere—maybe just outside the front entrance until she was done, if that was all right with her? Dr. S graciously gave them permission. As soon as they left, she pressed a complicated code into a keypad that was placed on the wall. A round metal door that had been completely camouflaged against the black metal swung open. Inside, on a metal tray, looking very small and frail, was the conch.

With a cry, Anand lunged forward and cupped it in his hands. He could feel its energy—but how weak it was, only a trickle. *I'm so glad to have found you!* he said silently.

I'm pretty happy about it myself, came the reply. *Whatever this vault—and the building—is made of, it drains magical objects. Let's get out of here.*

Anand unzipped his bodysuit and placed the conch carefully in an inside pocket. Away from the vault, it was growing stronger already. He could feel it pulsing against his skin like a second heart. Without further delay, the three of them made their way outside the building, where Dr. S informed the guards that the neutralizing procedure had been successful. Anand saw some of the guards eyeing the bucket, which he was carrying now, with curiosity. He stiffened, hoping no one would ask to take a look inside.

"Careful with that bucket!" Dr. S reprimanded him sharply. "Didn't I tell you that a reaction could still occur if you slosh the solution around? That's why we must remove it from the dome as soon as possible."

The guards fell back, and Dr. S marched briskly toward her white hover van. Anand noted, with some guilt, that the back doors did not close all the way. Dr. S strapped the bucket in with a belt and motioned for them to jump in.

"I hope you can repair the damage you caused to my doors, young man," she whispered as she slid into the driver's seat. "Otherwise, I'll have to answer to Dr. X—nothing escapes his eagle eye."

Abashed, Anand concentrated on the locking mechanism, but it was no use. His mind was too agitated to see into the essence of anything.

After a moment, however, he heard a smooth click. He stared at the locked doors in surprise. Then a smile broke over his face. The conch had fixed the doors for him. It must be regaining its power.

Before he could thank it, there was a banging on Dr. S's

window. It was the chief guard of the laboratory, his body-suit stiff with medals.

"Dr. S, I heard you're removing the—uh—volatile object from the dome. Where do you plan to take it?"

Dr. S looked offended at being questioned. "To Hazardous Dump 61, of course. It's the farthest from the city and therefore the safest."

"This means you'll have to travel across the slums, Doctor. I don't like that. You know how dangerous those slums are. I insist that you take a contingent of my best guards along. It would be terrible if you—and what you're carrying—fell into the wrong hands."

Anand's heart constricted. The presence of the guards would ruin all their plans.

Dr. S gave the man a condescending smile, though Anand could see a pulse beating nervously in her throat. "Because I appreciate the sense of duty that led to that remark, I will not take offense at your supposition that I am incapable of protecting myself. But I've been outside many times before. In fact, it wouldn't be wrong to say that I'm as much at home there as I am inside Futuredome. As for the object falling into the wrong hands, rest assured that I will do everything I can to prevent it."

Anand saw the guard's eyebrows draw together and wondered if the guard was aware of the double meaning behind her words. But before he could respond, Dr. S activated the hover van and backed smoothly out of the parking area.

WHAT S REMEMBERED

Anand had given a relieved sigh upon exiting the lab, but when the van approached the guard booth at the gates of Futuredome, where searchlights crisscrossed the dark of the artificial night, he grew nervous once again. Surely the plethora of machines at the gate would detect both the conch and the mirror. He cursed his stupidity. He should have asked Dr. S to drop them off near the wall in a deserted spot. With the help of the mirror, they could have passed through the wall and waited until she doubled back to pick them up. Now they were going to get caught, and all that he had worked so hard to achieve would be lost.

Conch, he called anxiously. *Maybe you should disguise yourself and the mirror. Or lay a spell on the guards so they don't notice anything strange when the machines start going crazy.*

There you go again, getting worked up over small things, the conch replied. *Wait and watch.*

At the gate, Dr. S repeated her story about the volatile object that needed to be removed to the dump, but now she added one more detail. Subjecting the object to rays from the search machines would probably cause it to blow up.

"If you intend to try such a risky procedure," she said, "I can't stop you. However, since this van, which is a property of the lab, is rather valuable, I'd rather you didn't jeopardize it—or myself and my assistants. Here's the sealed bucket with the object inside. You can carry it to the machine yourself. But wait until we back up a good distance. And if the machine gets damaged in the process, I want a written statement from you clarifying that I had advised against such an action."

The guard in charge, a young man with a fanatic's gleam in his eye, paused, weighing his options. Anand was afraid that in spite of Dr. S's warnings he would choose to pass the bucket through the machine. Then it would be a matter of minutes before he found out that the bucket contained nothing but water. But after a long moment the man nodded.

"Very well, Dr. S," he said. "I'll go by your expert advice. But I must follow procedure and report this entire incident to the Security Council before I allow you to leave the dome."

Dr. S gave a nonchalant nod, but Anand could see that same pulse beating at her neck. He guessed that if the council received the guard's message, they would order Dr. S to wait until someone came down to check on her highly irregular behavior.

The guard typed into something that looked like a small electric keypad. He punched a key several times, and then shook his head.

"Strange!" he said. "I can't seem to send the message. Something must be wrong with my Insta-communicator. And headquarters gave it to me just last month!"

"I'm afraid I can't wait around for you to fix your deficient equipment." Dr. S spoke with haughty impatience. "Every moment increases our risk."

The last statement was certainly true, Anand thought, though not in the way the guard understood it!

Dr. S revved the motor. "Open the gate," she said in a voice that was used to instant obedience. "Otherwise I'm the one who'll be sending a message to the Security Council about how you endangered the entire population of Futuredome."

Apologizing, the guard rushed to do as she ordered, and they were through.

***

The white van hurtled along the skyway, moving faster than normal. Glancing over at Dr. S, Anand saw that her fingers were gripping the controls so tightly that her knuckles were white. "I didn't think we would make it out," she said. "How lucky we were that the guard's communicator didn't work! Usually the gate guards get the best, most updated equipment."

Somehow, Anand didn't think it was mere luck. He sent a tendril of inquiry toward the conch and felt its aura of satisfaction.

"The conch helped you," he informed Dr. S.

She was so surprised that she turned to stare at him,

causing the van to wobble dangerously. "It can do that?"

"It can do a lot more," Anand said proudly. "If there's time later, I'll tell you of the many ways in which it has saved my life. Meanwhile, you might want to say a word of thanks. Objects of power appreciate politeness."

"Sorry!" Dr. S said, abashed. "I don't know much about these things." Her uncertain smile made her look younger and less severe. "Thank you, Conch. And you too, Mirror." She caressed the backpack lying beside her. "You gave me back something I thought I'd lost forever!"

Anand was curious as to what that was, but he did not wish to probe. From her tone, it seemed to be something private.

"I never thought I'd be this happy breathing brown air," Nisha said from behind her mask. "I take it that our destination isn't the Hazardous Dump. So where exactly are we going?"

Dr. S was silent. Then she said, "Into the past."

The white van took an exit off the skyway. Peering out into the muddy gloom, Anand noted with a start that they were deep in the slums. Around him, the shattered windows of derelict buildings looked like empty eye sockets.

Dr. S took the mirror out and consulted it again. Then she maneuvered her van closer to a building and turned off the engine. She jumped down lightly.

"I have to find something," she said. "I recommend you remain in the car. I'll turn on the security system. You'll be quite safe."

"You want to leave us out here alone?" Nisha said, staring at the dark ruins. "You must be joking!"

Once again, Anand caught a movement, quick and slippery, out of the corner of his eye, near a pile of rubble. Someone was watching them.

"We'll come with you," he said firmly.

Dr. S shrugged. "As you wish." From her backpack, she took out a cylinder and shook it. It began to glow. Stepping confidently into the narrow circle of light it projected, she strode toward the doorway of a skeletal structure that seemed as though it would collapse any moment. Anand and Nisha hastened to follow, stumbling over cracks in what had, long ago, been a sidewalk. What could Dr. S, a powerful scientist with a brilliant career, expect to find here, amidst piles of garbage?

All of a sudden, several figures materialized out of the darkness and surrounded Dr. S. Their silhouettes were lanky and their bodysuits torn in places, and in their hands they carried scavenged makeshift weapons—metal rods, legs from broken chairs, a handlebar from an old bicycle.

"What trouble are you making, science woman?" their leader demanded.

Anand and Nisha exchanged surprised glances. The voice was that of a teenage girl.

"Get away, white devil!" cried another figure, holding up a rod. He, too, sounded young. "We don't want you people here."

But a third one said, "Best if she don't go back and report on us. Let's grab her mask. She won't last long without it—and then we'll get a new bodysuit, plus whatever's in her pack." He motioned to the darkness, and a score of young people who had been camouflaged by it advanced menacingly upon Dr. S.

Anand's heart constricted with fear, but he forced himself to walk forward and stand beside the scientist. No matter what she had done, he could not stand by and watch her getting beaten up—or worse. He sent out a call to the conch, but it was strangely silent. He remembered the rule governing objects of power: They could not interfere in human affairs if there was a chance that the humans might be able to solve their own problem. But Nisha stepped up and stood by his side, her hands belligerently fisted.

The leader glared at them. "All this time we were feeling sorry for you, thinking you were her slaves. We were planning to set you free. Now it looks like we're going to get three bodysuits and three masks!"

If Dr. S was frightened, she didn't show it. "I'm searching for someone—people used to know her as Grandma Lila. Does she still live in Ganga Terrace?"

The leader peered suspiciously into her face. "How'd you know the name of that building? Except for a few old-timers, no one calls it that anymore, not since the guards came and tore it down years ago."

"I used to live there."

Dr. S's answer startled Anand even more than it did the gang leader. The pristine Dr. S had grown up *here*, in the slums of Kol? He had assumed that all scientists were born inside the domes.

"How do I know you're not lying?" the leader demanded.

"There were five Terrace buildings," Dr. S said. "They were named after rivers that used to flow through this continent a long time back. I had friends in Kaveri and Jamuna, though I've forgotten what the others were called."

"I don't know Grandma Lila," the leader said, her voice friendlier now. "But I can take you to Grandma Maya. She's one of the old-timers, too, and she lives close by." She ordered some of her companions to accompany them while the rest patrolled the area. Then she stared at Anand and Nisha. "If word gets out that people still live here, the city leaders will torch this entire place. *To clear it of vermin*, that's how they put it on the Pod. Can your assistants be trusted?"

"I would trust them with my life," Dr. S replied.

As he made his way unsteadily through the dark, Anand's whole body tingled with warmth at her reply.

൦ᢇᢇᢦ

The building the girl led them to could hardly be dignified by that name, though Anand could see that it had once been a large and prosperous apartment complex. Portions had collapsed, and the walls that still stood, with their brick and mortar exposed, were clearly unsafe. It reminded him of the ruins of Nawab Najib's palace—except this was worse.

141

There, the breeze had blown freely through the rubble, and the fallen roofs had been replaced by the starry sky. The wild creatures that inhabited the ruins lived, for the most part, in harmony with each other, all their needs met by the forest. But here he could hear the ominous skittering of claws in the dark, while the stench of urine assaulted his nostrils in spite of his mask. Down tunneled corridors, voices were raised in angry argument, and unfriendly faces watched them. Anand knew it was only their guide's stern gestures that held them back from falling upon Dr. S and her company and taking whatever they had. And how could Anand blame them? He noticed that the bodysuits of his escorts were tattered and too small, so that their bony wrists protruded from their sleeves. The tubes of their breathing masks were repaired with old tape, unraveling in places.

They approached the end of a corridor, dank and smelling of rot.

"Come," said their guide. She pushed aside a moldy, patched curtain and ushered them through what seemed like a hole. When Anand's eyes grew used to the gloom, he saw a bundle of rags on the floor. No, it was an old woman! Her chest made a whistling sound as she breathed laboriously.

The guide knelt and lit the stub of a candle. The care with which she performed this action made Anand realize what a precious commodity the lump of wax was.

"Grandma Maya!" The guide shook the woman gently. "Wake up! I've brought someone to see you."

"I'm tired of seeing people, young Ishani!" the woman said with a querulous cough. "I'd like to see some food instead—some real food, not the mush you folks have been feeding me the last hundred years! I want sweets like my mother used to make—curds thickened with jaggery, and red *pantuas* dipped in syrup."

"As I've told you, if I find some, you'll be the first to have it!" Ishani replied. "Now, here's a lady come to ask about the olden days that you love to go on and on about!"

The old woman peered at Dr. S. "But she's dressed like the white devils, Ishani," she said anxiously. "I don't think I should talk to her. She'll have me taken away to the Outlands."

"She's all right, Grandma," Ishani assured her. "She used to live here a long time ago, in Ganga Terrace."

"Don't be afraid." Dr. S spoke gently. "I just want to ask you about some people." She sat cross-legged on the floor, unmindful of the dirt, and rummaged in her pack. "I don't have the sweets you mentioned, but I do believe I have a bar of chocolate somewhere."

"I remember chocolate!" the old woman said. Her eyes shone greedily in the candlelight as she snatched the small bar Dr. S held out. "The first chocolates came from across the ocean. Then factories in Kol learned to make it. But then the factories were shut down, all except one, and only the white devils could have chocolate. Do you know, if you keep chocolate in your mouth long enough, it melts all over your tongue?"

Ishani and her companions watched the bar avidly. Anand could tell they longed to taste this almost-mythical substance. His own stomach growled with hunger.

"I wish I'd brought more," Dr. S said regretfully. "There's a whole boxful, sitting in my office. But I never thought—"

With shaking fingers, Grandma Maya unwrapped the bar. Anand thought she would pop it into her mouth, but she started breaking it up into miniscule pieces. She was going to share it with the young people around her, even though it meant she wouldn't get more than a tiny sliver herself.

"Wait!" Nisha said. She reached into her own pocket and took out the two bars she'd taken from Dr. S's office. Silently, she handed them to the old woman, who chuckled gleefully as she divided up the spoils. A smile broke out on Nisha's face as she watched the slum dwellers eat the chocolate. Anand found that—hungry though he was—he, too, was smiling.

"I haven't had chocolate in years!" Ishani said.

"I've never had it!" one of the younger boys remarked.

"Grandma Maya," Dr. S said, "I'm sorry to rush you, but I don't have much time. Did you know Grandma Lila and her family?"

The old woman nodded, licking the last bit of chocolate from her fingers.

"Lila and I and some of the other women used to make quilts together. These buildings were nicer then, in spite of the air starting to go brown. The magicians used to come by once in a while, secretly. They liked our quilts, and asked us to put good luck designs on for them. For payment they'd put a freshening spell on our windows so the air that blew through them wouldn't hurt our lungs."

"A freshening spell!" Anand whispered to Nisha. "That's why the magicians didn't need to wear masks inside the House of Fine Spirits."

"What happened to Lila?" Dr. S asked, her voice urgent. Grandma Maya continued as though she hadn't heard her.

"One day the white devils came. They weren't interested in our goods. It was our children they watched. They gave them fancy treats that we couldn't afford—potato chips and ice cream and even chocolate—and offered them new clothes if they would take a test. The ones that did really well on the test, the white devils took them away. How could we protest? They promised us the children would have a better life with them. Lila had a granddaughter, I forget her name. Mita or Asita—something like that. She was her only family. Her parents had died in one of the epidemics, but her grandma cared for her as best she could. Well, the devils got really excited when they saw her test results. They took the girl, promising Lila they'd bring her back any time she wanted to visit, but she never did return. She must have gotten used to all the good food and nice clothes."

Dr. S looked down at the ground. After a moment she said, "What happened to Lila? Was she sad?"

"Well, she wasn't around much longer herself," Grandma Maya said. "All the families whose children had been picked—the devils came back one day and took them all. Said the kids were sad without them, so they were going to have them live together inside the big dome they'd just built. But they didn't. One of the men managed to get back and tell us what happened. The scientists drove them far into the Outlands and took away their masks and suits and left them there. Most of them died in a day or so, from the bad air. The man who came back survived because he had picked up a few air-freshening techniques from the magicians, but he, too, died soon after. What did he have to live for?"

Dr. S had a tortured look on her face. "Oh, Grandma Maya, I didn't know any of this."

"The next time the white devils came to get more children," Grandma Maya continued, "our people put up a big fight. But the devils had those tubeguns. When they pointed them at you, it was like a million needles going through your bones. They had other machines that sent out an invisible force strong enough to bring down entire buildings. They destroyed the Terraces and killed most of the men. We had to run away and hide. We're still hiding—"

"They told us they'd taken our families to a better life in the Outer Lands," Dr. S whispered. "They said they had settled them in a new colony. When we finished our training, they said they'd take us to visit them. But then—I don't know what they did to us—we forgot, all of us. Futuredome became our whole world. The scientists became our families. What we were doing, to keep the domes going, seemed so important. We believed what they told us—that we were saving the world." Her voice grew stronger. "But now I know the truth. Now I see why Dr. X refused to give me permission to explore the Outer Lands. They were liars and murderers, and we children were their accomplices."

The old woman peered into Dr. S's face. "Who are you?"

Looking into her sorrowful eyes, Anand knew the answer before he heard it.

"My name is Sumita," Dr. S replied. "I'm Lila's granddaughter. But until a few hours ago, I didn't remember it."

Sumita sat very still in the white van, bent over the mirror. From time to time, tears rolled down her cheek. She did not wipe them away. Nisha sat by her, patting her shoulder awkwardly, murmuring consolations, but Sumita seemed unaware of her. Perhaps she was reliving the incidents she had been forced to forget for so many years. Or perhaps the mirror was showing her visions of her lost people. The sadness on her face made Anand feel hollow inside. A longing to help her rose in him, but he forced it aside. He had a greater responsibility. Even here, hidden in the depths of the slums, they were not safe. Any moment now, Dr. X would discover that the conch was missing. Then he would scour Kol with his Finder machines. Anand had to take the conch back to the Silver Valley before that happened. He was no longer angry with Sumita for her part in the devastation, but he could not—as the hermit had warned him—afford to get embroiled in her problems.

"Dr.—uh—Sumita," he said, "I thank you for helping us bring the conch safely out of Futuredome. But now we—and the conch—must return to the valley and try to set it to rights. The mirror, too, must be sent back to its rightful home."

Sumita did not look up. She just clutched the mirror tighter.

"We can't leave her like this," Nisha whispered to Anand. "She's in shock. If the scientists find her and realize that she took the conch from the vault, I don't know what they'll do to her."

"But if we stay here, they'll recapture the conch—and us, too. We can't fight them. Their machines are too strong. You've seen it yourself."

Nisha scrunched up her forehead, the way she did when she was thinking very hard. When she opened her eyes, they shone with excitement. "Let's take Sumita back to the valley with us. She's smart and hard working—and a good person besides. She could become an herb healer like me!"

"Are you crazy?" Anand cried. "Have you forgotten that she's the one who caused all the damage in the first place? The healers would never accept her."

"I'll talk to Master Somdatta myself," Nisha insisted. "I'll explain to him that without her we wouldn't have been able to recover the conch. Please! We can't just abandon her."

Anand, too, felt guilty about leaving Sumita to face her fate, but he still had misgivings. Even if she were accepted by the Brotherhood, could Sumita be happy in the valley, where life was so different from everything she had known?

Conch, he inquired. *Is this the right thing to do?* But the conch did not answer.

Time was seeping away, like water through a cupped hand. Every moment of indecision increased their danger. Anand pushed aside his doubts. "Come with us," he said to Sumita.

Nisha touched the scientist's face with gentle fingers. "You can stay with me in the women's hut and learn about the healing herbs from Mother Amita. We'll be like sisters. You'll be able to use your skills to help many people." When Sumita did not respond, she added, "There's nothing left for you here."

Sumita took in a deep, shuddering breath. "You're right," she said. She did not look at Nisha but gazed vacantly over her shoulder. "There's nothing for me here, in this world that we've divided and destroyed with our greed. I might as well go with you."

"That's decided then," Anand said with some relief, although he was disappointed that Sumita did not sound more enthusiastic. He took out the conch, wondering again why it had not responded to his question.

"Please, Conch," he said, "let's go home."

THE ANNOUNCEMENT

Anand felt the conch come to life in his hand, vibrating faintly. From previous experience he knew that the vibration would increase. Then the conch would send out a dazzling radiance, an energy field within which it would envelop them before transporting them where they wanted to go.

"Quick!" he called to Nisha and Sumita. "We have to hold hands."

But Sumita was staring as though hypnotized at the small sphere on the dashboard of the van, a miniature version of the Pods Anand had seen at the party. A red light had begun to flash from it.

"A red message on the Pod!" she said. "That's the highest urgency level. I've got to see what it is."

Nisha pulled at her arm. "Don't!" she said. "Let's just leave. You yourself agreed there's nothing for you here."

But already a hologram had formed above the sphere. A woman in an official-looking purple bodysuit announced, "All citizens on the alert! As you know from our last Pod-flash, a group of magicians broke into the main laboratory of Futuredome a few hours earlier. They stole an extremely hazardous energetic object that the scientists had procured with great difficulty to fuel the machines that keep Kol alive. With this act of sabotage, the magicians have placed all our lives in danger. Additionally, they have kidnapped Dr. S, the senior scientist in charge of the lab. No one knows what they've done to her."

A hologram of Sumita, frowning sternly, hovered above the sphere, and then disintegrated, to be replaced by an image of Dr. X.

"The esteemed Dr. X, creator of the X-Converter, without which this city would have been doomed long ago, has sent an ultimatum to the magicians," the announcer continued. "If the saboteurs do not return the energetic object to Futuredome within twenty-four hours, all imprisoned magicians will be executed publicly, in the Maidan. He has also announced a reward for anyone who can provide information regarding the whereabouts of Dr. S. And now, here is a response from the magicians—"

A hologram of Commandant Vijay wavered above the Pod. Whoever had created it had taken pains to make it particularly unflattering. He looked gaunt and hungry, with red-rimmed eyes and unkempt hair that flew madly about his face. "We didn't do it!" he shouted. "The scientists messed things up once again, and they're trying to frame us! But this much is certain: If they harm even one of our people, it's out-and-out war. This time we won't stop until they're destroyed, even if that means—"

He was cut off in mid-sentence. The announcer, looking harried, stated, "Anyone who has information that might help the Security Council deal with this volatile situation is urged to activate the contact button on your Pod and speak with us immediately."

With a click, the Podsphere turned itself off, leaving the three people in the car in stunned silence.

ᏨᢏᏍᎽᏞ

Anand was the first to speak. "I wish we hadn't heard that!" he said with a sigh. In his mind he saw Basant's earnest face. If it hadn't been for his advice, Nisha and he might still be stuck inside the rehabitational. He remembered Basant's mother, too. Just before they had left the magicians' den, she'd grasped both his hands in hers.

"I hope you find your object of power," she had said. "Please ask it to help us bring our prisoners home."

What would she say now, if she knew that Anand was the one responsible for this execution order?

"I'm sorry!" Sumita said. "I shouldn't have listened to the Pod. But it's an old habit, dinned into our heads from the time the scientists brought us to the dome. The two of you should go back to your world. Once you're safely away, I'll turn myself in and take the blame for the loss of the conch. That'll stop the scientists and magicians from fighting."

It would be so simple to just say yes, Anand thought. He

longed to leave this mess to those who had created it. But he shook his head. "I can't let them punish you for something we asked you to do. Besides, Dr. X won't believe you— especially since you won't have any proof. He'll still blame it on the magicians, claiming they somehow forced you to steal the conch. It'll give him the perfect excuse to destroy them. No, we have to stay." Regretfully, he replaced the conch inside his shirt. As it left his hand, he felt warmth pooling into his palm, as though the conch approved of his choice.

"But how can we help Sister Sumita?" Nisha asked.

Anand said, "Our best bet is to meet with the scientists and the magicians, both groups at once. We've got to make them see the madness of what they're doing, using up their resources to attack each other when they need to band together to help Kol."

Sumita gave a short, mirthless laugh. "You're the one who's mad, to think they'll listen! They won't even bother to meet with you."

"They will if they know I have the conch."

"If you take the conch to them," Sumita replied, "you'll cause an even bigger fight as each group tries to gain control of it. And whoever gets it will use it against the other faction. No. It's best you leave. We're beyond helping here."

Nisha looked apprehensive, but she said, "No one is beyond helping. That was one of the first things they taught us in the valley. And sometimes, just by trying to help, we change the situation. Don't worry about us. Remember, we have the conch. Just its presence will make us more powerful than the scientists and magicians combined."

About time someone gave me a little credit! The conch's beloved, wry voice sounded in Anand's ear. *You're right about trying to get everyone together. Ask the scientists and magicians to meet you for negotiations in the Maidan tomorrow. Tell them to come to the center of the field, to the raised platform where in older times concerts were performed. They must be there by noon.*

Noon? Anand said uncertainly. *But it's almost morning already! That leaves us only a few hours.*

Noon is when my power is at its fullest, the conch said, *and I'll need that. This place where air and earth have turned to poison saps my energy.*

What if they refuse to come?

Tell them you'll demonstrate my power. That'll entice them. Invite as many of the common people of Kol as you can gather. Demand that the prisoners be brought there, too. If a lasting solution is to be worked out, everyone must be present.

I'm so glad you'll be there to make them do what's right, Anand said in relief.

Whatever gave you such an idea? the conch said. *My job is merely to provide you with a barrier of safety so no one can attack you. You're the ones who'll have to convince all those pigheaded people to cooperate, you and Miss Impatience and that weepy scientist woman.*

Things moved rapidly after that. Once Anand told her what the conch wanted, Sumita activated the Pod and sent out a message urging all citizens to join them for the meeting at the Maidan. She invited scientists and magicians and councilmen, addressing each group separately. "If you come with an open mind," she said, "I promise to show you something so amazing that it'll change your life."

Hoping they had access to a Pod somewhere in the Terraces, she invited Ishani and the teenagers that roamed the ruins and asked them to bring all their friends. "I want your voice in the decision we make," she said.

She even pleaded with the guards at the rehabitationals to bring their prisoners. "We're offering you the hope of a world where your only contact with people won't be to stun them with your Electrotubes," she told them, speaking as earnestly as she could. "Wouldn't you like it if people were actually happy to see you?

"I hope the Podcasters will relay the messages," she said to Anand and Nisha after she had finished speaking into the pod.

"I think they will—it's bound to be the most sensational piece of news they have!" Nisha replied.

"Now we need to get away from the van as quickly as possible," Sumita said. "Once the Pod's messenger system is activated, the Finder machines can locate it in a matter of minutes. Then the Security Council will surely—"

Before she could finish her sentence, the Pod began to flash. This time the light was a soothing blue, pulsing in a particular rhythm. Sumita's mouth set in an angry line as she watched it.

"That's Dr. X's personal code," she said. "That was quick!"

"Don't listen to him," Nisha said. "It isn't safe to stay here any longer—you said so yourself."

But Dr. X had already started speaking, his voice deep and mellifluous and oddly riveting.

"My dear S!" he cried. "I can't tell you how thankful I was to hear your voice! At least you're alive—even though from your message it sounds like the magicians still have you in their power. Will they allow you to speak to me?"

"No one's stopping me from doing anything," Sumita said. "I'm here of my own will."

There was a pause. "I can't believe that," Dr. X said. "They must have put a Hypnospell on you."

Anand and Nisha had jumped down from the van. "Come on," Anand whispered, tapping Sumita's shoulder, but she was totally focused on the Pod.

"No Hypnospell here," she said in a hard, bitter voice. "But maybe I'm just waking from one—the one that you and your cohorts put on us children when you took us from the slums so that we'd forget our people. So that we wouldn't ask any inconvenient questions when you sent them away to die."

There was the slightest of pauses. Then Dr. X said, "That's not how it was. Don't you remember the personal interest I took in you ever since you came to live in Future-dome? Didn't I make sure you always got the best—from food to clothing to the latest equipment for your schooling and then your research? Why, I loved you like my own child!"

Nisha pulled at Sumita's arm. "Come on! Don't talk to him anymore!"

Sumita flicked her hand away. "Don't use that word!" she cried into the Pod, her voice shaking. "You don't even know what love is, you and your colleagues. You did your best to cut all loving out of us. You pitted us children against each other so we saw the others only as rivals for your attention. And as for taking care of me, you did that merely because I was good with machines. You used me."

"Calm down, my dear," Dr. X's voice soothed. "You've misinterpreted the facts. Once I see you face-to-face, I promise to clarify everything to your satisfaction. You'll see then that everything I did was for the good of Kol. Just stay where you are and I'll send my own personal hovercopter to pick you up. Uh—do you still have the object in your possession?"

"That's what you're really interested in, isn't it?" Sumita said through clenched teeth. "Yes, I have it. And I'll die before I hand it over to you!"

"That would be a pity," said Dr. X, his voice mournful.

There was no sound, but some sixth sense made Anand look up into the night sky. Hovering directly above them was an aircraft shaped like a disc. The guards must have traced the conversation and taken up their position while Dr. X distracted Sumita. Something black and diaphanous fell from the disc, widening into a huge circle.

"It's a net!" Nisha cried.

Anand grabbed Sumita's backpack and pulled her from the van. "We've got to get to the Terraces," he shouted. "They're our only hope. Once we're in the corridors, we can hide. Maybe Ishani and the others can help us."

The three of them sprinted toward the ruins, which were, fortunately, not far. Anand thought they had a good chance of reaching them. But then, glancing over his shoulder as they fled, he saw that the net was larger than it had first appeared. Perhaps it was equipped with sensors, for instead of falling straight down, it glided swiftly toward them. Now it was only a few feet above their heads. Worse, guards equipped with parachutes were jumping from a door that had opened up on the bottom of the aircraft. Tubeguns gleamed in their hands as they floated down lazily, not bothering to hurry.

Anand ran until his lungs felt as though they would burst. He could hear Sumita and Nisha panting close behind. The dark silhouette of the Terrace was only a few paces away. They had made it! He ducked into a doorway and leaned his head against the jamb, panting.

Just then Nisha fell to the ground with a grunt of pain. In her hurry, she must have tripped on a chunk of rubble. As Anand watched in horror, the net dropped over her.

"Keep going!" she shouted. "Save the conch and the mirror!"

Anand had thought he couldn't move another inch, but a wave of strength surged over him as he saw his friend struggling with the net. There was something strange about the net, for her struggles slowed and finally ceased. He rushed back to her. Behind him, he could hear Sumita shouting something, but he ignored her. He grabbed the net, trying to lift it off Nisha. It was very heavy—and sticky, like a monster spider web. Now both he and Nisha were stuck to it.

No wonder the guards hadn't needed to hurry!

"It's an Adhesa-web!" Sumita, who had reached them, said. "That's what I was trying to warn you about." She pulled out a pocketknife and sawed at the netting around them, careful not to get her hands entangled. But though the netting looked delicate, it was amazingly tough. She could barely cut through a strand. There was no way she would be able to free them in time.

Nisha twisted her head to look up at Anand, tears of frustration on her cheeks. "I'm so sorry! I've ruined it all. You shouldn't have come back."

"Don't be silly," Anand said. In his head he added, *We live or die together.* He pressed a finger against the web and clumsily wiped the tears from her cheeks. Even in the midst of the great danger he was facing, his heart expanded. He did not want to move his eyes away from her dirt-streaked, beautiful face.

"They're on the ground," Sumita whispered. "They'll be on us in a few seconds." Her face was full of despair, and she dropped the knife. It struck Anand that, being a scientist, she knew exactly what the guards would do to their victims.

Conch! he called in despair. *Help us!*

The answer reverberated in his chest like a thundercloud. *Foolish boy! To trust your safety to those weak, stumbling human legs when all the time you carried the gateway on your back!*

The gateway? On my back? thought Anand, confused, then realized that Sumita's backpack was slung over his shoulder.

"Quick!" he cried to Sumita. "Pull out the mirror. Press it against the net so that we can all touch it." A part of him quailed with doubt. What if he was wrong and the mirror, too, got stuck to the net?

The guards were close now. Seeing that Anand was up to something, the leader barked an order to his men and they broke into a jog, tubes aimed and ready. Frantically, Anand gabbled a protection spell. He was sure that in his panic he had left out a crucial line, but he felt a sudden heaviness behind him, as though a thick curtain had fallen. Had the conch come to his rescue?

Nisha and he had each managed to push some part of their body against the mirror, which Sumita was holding.

Would it work? In the past, in order to use the mirror, they had had to place both feet firmly on it. But he had no option. "Activate the jammer!" he heard the leader yell. A high whining filled the air, boring into his skull. The pain made him want to scream. It was hard to keep anything in his head, image or thought or word. For a moment he could not even remember what he was trying to do. Already the protection spell was fraying. He felt a muffled blast from a tubegun pierce his shoulder like an angry javelin.

With the last of his breath, he cried, "Mirror, please, take us somewhere safe!"

Immediately he was sucked into a lightless, airless tunnel. He couldn't breathe or hear. He couldn't see his companions. He put out a hand, but there was no one beside him. He could feel his body tumbling head over heels—falling or rising, he couldn't tell which. A great weight pushed at him from every side until he thought he would implode. No. He was in a vacuum. His limbs floated, expanding, until they were as insubstantial as clouds.

Suddenly, all around him, a light bloomed, so bright that it hurt his eyes. He sensed that he was lying on something soft and white. Was this heaven? Was that how the mirror had interpreted his desire to go someplace safe? Was he dead, then? If this was how good death felt, he did not mind it.

He pulled off his mask, sensing that he did not need it here. He took a deep breath, massaging the lines it had pressed into his face. There was a delicious smell around him, like fresh, ripe fruit. Mangoes? He wanted to find them, but first he needed to discover where the light was coming from. Turning his head, he found himself looking out of a large window at the sun. There was a plant on the sill, buds peeping from between its glossy leaves. One of them had opened into a flower. He knew its name, *aparajita*, the unconquerable. As he gazed at the thin, silky petals, deep blue with purple centers, he realized where the mirror had brought them.

"This isn't heaven," he said. "It's Sumita's apartment."

FRIENDS

"I take it back!" said Anand as he sat at the dining table, dressed in a clean white bodysuit, fresh from the first shower he had taken since he'd left the Silver Valley for the hermit's cave. "This *is* heaven."

"Mmm!" Nisha agreed, her mouth full. "These fried eggs are certainly fit for the gods."

"Heaven, yes. That's what I, too, thought when they first gave me this apartment." Sumita's smile was bitter. "What could be better than a place of one's own, furnished with every gadget a scientist could imagine, clean clothes to wear, real food from the Farm instead of tiny portions of mutated mush, sunlight—even if it was artificial—and air that you didn't have to look at as you breathed it?" She must have been as hungry as Anand and Nisha, but she pushed her eggs around on her plate. "Only now I'm realizing the cost—to others and to myself. Only now I'm realizing what a fool I was, what a willing pawn in X's hands."

"Don't be so hard on yourself," Nisha said. "You were only a child when he took you from your family. I know—

because I lived on the streets myself—how terrible life can look when your stomach is empty, and how grateful you can feel toward anyone who fills it."

"I can't forgive myself so easily," Sumita started to say, but just then the Pod on her side table sputtered to life. The announcer pulled nervously at the neck of his bodysuit as he spoke.

"The scientists have decided to ignore the earlier message urging a meeting of all the major groups that inhabit Kol. Dr. X has expressed serious doubts about its authenticity."

Dr. X's hologram radiated concern. "I've known Dr. S ever since she was a child. She was one of my most brilliant protégés. She would never voice such treacherous sentiments. The magicians who kidnapped her have clearly damaged her mind. We must, therefore, proceed with our original plan of quelling these insurgents, and do it so thoroughly that such an incident never recurs."

The announcer reappeared, looking unhappy. "Due to the volatile atmosphere of Kol, the Security Council has decided to have the prisoners executed privately inside the various rehabitation facilities tomorrow morning. Images of the executions will be Podflashed to all citizens throughout the day. The magicians have responded to this decision with a serious threat of their own."

Now the Pod projected a hologram of the commandant, his jaw set, his fist raised. "With each execution, we will undertake retaliatory executions of our own!"

The hologram vanished.

"I knew they wouldn't agree!" Sumita cried passionately. "They're too selfish. Too shortsighted."

Anand paced up and down, trying to think of a way to break this gridlock. "Do you have personal friends among the scientists? Maybe you could talk to them individually, explain about the conch and the mirror; ask them to persuade their friends to come to the Maidan. All we need is one meeting—"

Sumita gave a harsh laugh. "Didn't you hear me earlier? I don't have any friends. None of us do. That's how we survived inside Futuredome. That's what we were taught—to always be at each others' throats, to betray each other for the slightest chance of gaining X's favor."

Nisha had been quiet all this while, but now she said, "Why don't you look in the mirror, Sister Sumita? It has shown you so many valuable things. Perhaps it will suggest a solution."

But when Sumita looked into the mirror, she gave a disbelieving gasp. "If anyone else had suggested this," she said, "I would have said he was crazy."

"Who did you see?" Nisha asked.

"Dr. A!"

Anand remembered the haughty woman at the party who had accused Sumita of voicing treacherous sentiments.

"She's my biggest rival," Sumita continued. "My arch

enemy. We came to Futuredome around the same time. Ever since then she's been trying to outmaneuver me and become X's favorite. We rarely have a conversation that doesn't end in an argument. But the mirror insists that she's the one I need to contact, so I guess I'll have to swallow my pride and do it."

She picked up her Insta-communicator and began typing into it. In a moment, however, she looked up, her face drawn. "The message won't go through. X must have had my communicator neutralized." She hurried to the table and lifted a small gadget to her ear. "My Electrafone's dead, too!" she said, throwing it down. "He has cut me off from everyone! Only the Pod works, but as soon as I use it, he'll know where I am. And you've already seen how rapidly those guards move." Tears of helpless rage sprang to her eyes.

Nisha watched the door of the apartment as though at any moment guards might burst through it. "What'll we do now, Anand?"

But all Anand could think was that the window of time left for returning to the valley was rapidly shrinking.

Well, for one thing, you could all calm down, the conch said with some asperity. *You humans—always so excitable! Anand, could you perhaps get the scientist woman to stop crying? I've observed that she has a tendency to weep at the drop of a hat—or should I say phone? Once she's managed that, tell her to hold me as she turns on the Pod. I'll provide a shield so no one*

can overhear or locate her. By the way, I'd appreciate it if she
doesn't get any tears on me. They tend to corrode my shell.

In the hologram that appeared over the Pod, Dr. A stared at
Sumita, flabbergasted.

"I can't believe you called me on the Pod, S! You must be
even stupider than I thought all these years. Don't you know
they're scouring Kol—up, down, and sideways—looking
for you? Dr. X has declared a Level 16 emergency, stating
that you have a hazardous weapon that could blow up all the
domes at once. The public has been told that you've been
kidnapped, but Dr. X called a private meeting of the top
scientists—I was included, of course—where he informed
us you've defected and gone over to the magicians. He also
promised a hefty reward to anyone who can give them news
of your whereabouts."

"Are you going to do that, A?" Sumita asked softly. "Are
you going to turn me in?"

"I should—but I don't have to! Every Finder in the
system is already tuned in to the Pod frequency. In about
three minutes, guards will be gift-wrapping you in Adhesa-
web. By this time tomorrow I'll be inheriting your office—
and your projects."

"You're welcome to them," Sumita said. "I have no
intention of going back to the lab."

"Why did you Pod me then?" Dr. A asked, looking suspicious. "Are you trying to entangle me in your troubles so

you can take me down with you?" She stood up and raised her right hand and announced, "I hereby declare that I have nothing to do with S's seditions and in fact am turning my Pod off right now."

"Dramatic as always!" Sumita said. "Don't worry. No one's listening in on our conversation because I have a shield around us. No, don't ask me what kind of shield, because I can't explain it. I want to show you something, though— the hazardous weapon X has warned everyone of." She held up her palm with the conch in it.

Dr. A squinted, craning her neck. "That's a dwarf-sized *strombus gigas*, if I'm not mistaken," she said in an irritated voice. "Long extinct and quite useless. S, are you playing mind games with me?"

Long extinct? Quite useless? Anand heard the conch say indignantly.

"No, Asha," Sumita said. "I'm showing you what almost no one now living in Kol has seen—a magical conch, an object of the greatest power, though it is a power that heals instead of causing destruction. It is what placed the protective shield around me."

Anand expected Dr. A to scoff at the notion of a magical conch, but she seemed to not have fully registered what Sumita said. A look—half wonder, half shock—had come over her face.

"What did you call me?" she whispered.

"I called you Asha, the name your parents gave you."

"I had forgotten!" Dr. A's voice was a mere whisper.

"The name I used to call you by when we lived in the Terraces and played together," Sumita added.

"The Terraces! And my little brother, who always used to make a pest of himself by tagging along with us! How could I have forgotten him?"

"I too had forgotten everything—even my grandmother whom I loved best in all the world—until the mirror, another magical object I hope to show you sometime, helped me to remember."

"I never did go to the Outer Lands to see them, like I'd promised my little brother," Dr. A said, biting her lip. "What must he have thought of me!"

"Don't blame yourself," Sumita said. "X and his team tampered with our memories. It would have done us no good to go there anyway." Succinctly, she told Dr. A how their families were taken outside the boundaries of Kol and left there to die. "I'm sorry to break this terrible news to you," she added, "but I needed you to know the truth about X. You've got to help me foil his plans. You have to pass on this information to the other scientists who were brought in from the outside like us."

"What if they don't believe me?"

"Tell them their birth names."

"But how will I know those?"

"They'll come back to you, as yours did to me. Urge the scientists to come to the meeting at the Maidan at noon.

Once you get them to agree, announce it on the Pod. This will encourage the magicians to come, too. The meeting is our only chance of changing things: of removing X from power, of working together with the magicians to save our world, of making sure our families didn't die for nothing."

There was a new determination on Dr. A's face. "Then I'll do it! You can count on me, Sumita. I can't promise I'll be successful, but I'll try my best."

Sumita's hands were shaking as she switched off the Pod. "I never thought she'd listen." She cupped the conch in her palm. "Thank you, Conch! Every time I got angry at something Asha said, I could feel you sending me the strength to remain calm. But you did something else, too. As I spoke, I could sense the jealousy I'd held on to all these years draining away. I felt, instead, how scared she must have been when she was brought here—just like me. Thank you for that!" She lifted the conch to her lips and kissed it. "No matter what happens, I'll treasure this gift the rest of my life."

Yechh! said the conch. *Didn't anyone ever tell her that saliva dulls our sheen?*

But Anand guessed that it was pleased.

"I suppose there's nothing to do now except listen to Podflashes and hope the scientists decide to come to the summit," said Nisha. "Well, as long as we're waiting, Sister Sumita—do you have any more of those scrumptious fried eggs?"

SHOWDOWN

It was almost noon when Anand threaded his nervous way through the ragtag crowd that had gathered in the Maidan. If he had not known it to be the same park he used to visit on holiday afternoons with his family, Anand would never have recognized it. Gone was the grass, stretching as far as his child eyes could see, on which he had sat with his parents, eating old-woman's-hair candy that turned his mouth a sticky pink. Gone were the Krishna Chura trees that dropped red flowers on the walkways. Gone were the vendors of hot snacks and the balloon makers who twisted long colorful balloons into animal shapes. Now the Maidan was barren, its earth so dry that it had cracked into deep chasms that Anand had to navigate cautiously. And the people surrounding him—mostly the slum dwellers of Kol—were a grim and silent lot. Dressed in patched bodysuits and taped-up masks, they looked around distrustfully, as though they expected a horde of guards to materialize and arrest them. Still, they had responded to Sumita's appeal and emerged from the mazes of the Terraces to attend the summit. That,

Anand thought, adjusting his own mask carefully to hide as much of his face as possible, was a victory in itself.

Anand was wearing one of Sumita's discarded bodysuits, which she had found in her rag box. For good measure, she'd ripped one of the sleeves before giving it to him and rubbed some grease onto it as well. She'd done the same with her own bodysuit and Nisha's. Once the mirror had transported them to a side street choked by garbage, she suggested that they each move separately toward the center of the Maidan.

"I'm sure the guards from the laboratory have informed the Security Council that we are a group of three," she said. "That's what they'll be looking for. Alone, we each have a better chance of reaching the platform."

The thought of separating made Anand anxious. What if the crowds stampeded and they lost each other? What if one of them was caught—Sumita most likely, as everyone must have seen her hologram on the Pod? What if someone snatched the mirror, which she was carrying in a backpack? How could Anand help her if he was far away? And Nisha—he worried about her most of all. Sumita had the mirror and Anand the conch, but she would have no magical object to protect her. However, he could not come up with a better suggestion, so he agreed reluctantly.

"Stay close to the platform," Sumita instructed, "but don't reveal yourself until I give you the signal. We'll climb onto the platform at the same time." She ducked into the crowd, and so did Nisha. Anand tried to keep them in his sight as he pushed his way through the throng, but the beating of drums distracted him. A procession was making its way to the platform, figures with once-bright cloaks draped over their bodysuits, accompanied by musicians. The men wore turbans on their heads. The women's arms jangled with cheap bracelets, and above their breathing masks their eyes were boldly painted in many colors. The magicians had arrived, dressed in their finery—whatever was left of it— and they wanted to make sure everyone noticed them.

"It's the spell casters," a man in the crowd shouted, and others took up the cry, some calling it out in awe and some with suspicion. Anand surmised that their responses depended on whether they had known the magicians personally, or had only heard of their reputation on Podflashes. In any case, several people backed away from the platform, and Anand made use of this opportunity to edge forward until he was close enough to overhear the magicians' conversation.

Chief Deepak led his people onto the platform, where they seated themselves cross-legged along one side, all except Vijay, who paced up and down, his worn but elegant blue cloak swishing around him. "It is almost noon," he cried. "Where are those vermin? The prisoners aren't here, either." He scowled at his uncle. "You should have taken my advice and remained home. This is a trap to capture our entire clan all at once."

The chief, who looked frailer than ever, said something in a placating voice, but Vijay retorted, "If we go down, we'll take as many of them with us as we can!"

Basant's mother, wrapped in a faded maroon shawl, sat to one side of the platform, her eyes restlessly combing the crowd. Anand knew she was looking for her son. He, too, searched the crowd with a sinking heart. There was no sign of the guards from the rehabitationals. They had decided not to risk bringing the prisoners out.

Vijay stood up angrily. "This is an insult to us, and unsafe besides, to sit and wait here, easy targets for the guards, who are in the scientists' pay. I insist—"

But the rest of his words were lost in a giant roar. A fleet of blood-red bullet cars sped down the middle of the Maidan, scattering a terrified crowd—for everyone knew to whom these cars belonged. The magicians jumped to their feet, their faces drawn. Several of them reached inside their cloaks, and Anand realized that they had not come unarmed. He stiffened. Was the summit he'd pinned all his hopes on going to turn into a blood bath before it even started?

Please, Conch, he implored. *Do something to calm them down.*

Then he heard Basant's mother give a cry. The doors of the bullet cars had swung up and prisoners were stumbling from them. They looked thin and scruffy, with long, unkempt hair, and they were handcuffed and collared, but otherwise they appeared unhurt. The magicians on the platform exclaimed as they recognized family members they had not seen in months. Many of them wept. Some tried to jump down and go to their loved ones and had to be restrained. The prisoners raised their handcuffed arms in greeting, though their collars prevented them from speaking.

"Stay alert!" Vijay cried as more bullet cars arrived—and still more, until Anand thought every guard in Kol must be here. The guards jumped out and surrounded the prisoners. Some aimed their tubeguns at them while others kept a wary eye on the magicians. Still others watched the slum dwellers, who had retreated even farther at the sight of those deadly blue cylinders. The message was clear: The guards had come, yes, but they didn't trust anyone. At the first sign of trouble, they would ruthlessly squash those who were responsible for it.

I feel like I'm inside a pot that's about to boil over, Anand told the conch.

Focusing on the worst again, I see, the conch quipped.

The conch was right. It was a giant step for the guards to decide to join the summit. Anand knew he should be delighted that they had been persuaded by Sumita's message to bring the prisoners with them. The presence of the prisoners would keep the magicians calm; they would not want to do anything to jeopardize their dear ones.

He only wished he could see Sumita. And Nisha—where was she?

He heard an angry buzz, like the sound of a giant alarm clock, and then a booming voice rose from all around him. He had not noticed that Pods were positioned throughout the Maidan. The hologram of a sign announcing that it was noon flashed from them. The buzzing grew into a roar, and a wind swept dust into Anand's eyes. Where could it have come from? Winds had stopped blowing in Kol a long time ago.

Then he saw the hovercopters, dazzling white, landing in the field behind the platform. Asha had managed to convince the scientists to join the summit!

The scientists climbed onto the platform single file, Dr. X in the lead, his head regally high, his face radiating disapproval. Anand could hear the murmurs from the crowd, part angry, part admiring. People were afraid of the scientists, yes. But they held them in great awe, too. They had grown up believing that it was the scientists' constant, untiring work that kept their world from collapsing. Could they muster the strength to stand up against them if necessary?

When the scientists reached their side of the platform, they each took out a small box and pressed a series of buttons. Cogs chugged. The boxes opened, metamorphosing themselves into stools on which the scientists sat, looming over the magicians. The magicians muttered at this discourtesy, but the scientists ignored them.

Anand's eyes caught a movement near the platform steps. It was Sumita, but instead of following the plan she had sketched out, she began running up the steps on her own. What was she thinking of, taking such a risk? Anand pushed past people as fast as he could. He was certain that any

moment Sumita would be attacked—and overpowered—
by guards, but to his surprise she climbed onto the platform
unhindered and stood facing Dr. X. But he himself had
barely set foot on the stairs when a contingent of guards who
had been concealed behind an overhang rushed up and surrounded him. At least twenty blue cylinders pointed at his chest.
The crowds around him shrank back. Though some of
them looked at him pityingly, no one dared to get mixed up
in guard business. Behind him, Anand heard a piercing cry.
Wheeling, he saw Nisha running headlong toward him. But
she didn't get anywhere close. A new contingent of guards
materialized from behind the overhang and cut her off.

Anand called out to Sumita, but her attention was focused
on Dr. X and she didn't hear him. Or did she choose to
ignore his cry for help? Had she planned this all along? Misgiving filled Anand's mouth with bitterness as he wondered
if she had merely used him and Nisha—and their connection
with the objects of power—to get herself here.

The leader of the guards prodded him with his tubegun,
indicating that Anand should climb onto the stage. Nisha,
too, was being pushed up the stairs. He ascended the steps
reluctantly, aware of the prick of a thousand curious eyes
from the crowd. Ahead, the scientists glared at him. To them
he was a dangerous rogue who wanted to destroy the civi-
lization they had built with a lifetime of effort. From the
other side of the platform, the magicians' eyes bored into
him. No doubt Vijay had embellished the incident where

Nisha and Anand had escaped from him with the mirror. They thought of him as a hotheaded fool who would now be forced to give up the treasure that might have saved them all. Around him stood the impassive-faced guards, who, he was sure, would like nothing better than to drag him to a rehabilitational—this time for a permanent stay. He tried to catch Sumita's eye, but she was staring at Dr. X, that telltale pulse beating once again in her neck. Anand's heart sank. How had he ever believed that he could persuade all these people, sworn enemies each focused on their own interests, to reconcile?

ɔ✿c

"Ah, here you are, my dear S," Dr. X said with an affable smile. "I'm very happy to see that you are safe!" He came forward as though to give her a hug, but Sumita stepped back, and he was left standing with arms outstretched. An expression of rage flashed over his face for a moment, and then was replaced by another smile.

Sumita clutched the backpack holding the mirror tightly to her chest and watched him warily.

"I take it that backpack contains the object we discussed in our most enjoyable conversation a few hours ago? I'm glad you had the intelligence to bring it with you—but then, you were always bright. This will make our job far easier." Dr. X's voice dropped intimately, as though he and Sumita were having a private conversation. Anand suspected that he was using Persuasion again and didn't want the assembly—particularly the magicians—to hear him. "The best option—and the most comfortable for you—would be to hand it over to me peacefully. Such cooperation will make it clear to all that you had been Hypnospelled by the magicians. I'll get rid of your 'helpers' discreetly—I guess that's who those two Illegals standing behind you are. Once we harvest the object, I'll promote you to second in command, changing your official designation to S-2, and we can all forget this unpleasant episode."

Anand could see Sumita hesitating. He clenched his fists, afraid to hear her reply. It was a perilously tempting offer on so many levels. Safety, power, riches, prestige: How could he expect her to turn them all down in favor of a precarious, seesawing future?

"You can even focus your research on the Outer Lands, like you've been wanting to," Dr. X added with a benevolent smile.

But here he had made a crucial tactical error. Sumita's entire body stiffened, and she held up a pendant hanging around her neck. It must have been a microphone of some kind, for when she spoke, her voice came out magnified. "The same Outer Lands to which you sent my grandmother and A's parents and little brother, and the families of half the scientists present here today," she asked, her voice dangerously smooth, "so that they would die there? You did it so they wouldn't ask inconvenient questions or badger you to send us home, didn't you? And then you tampered with our memories so we wouldn't remember them. So you could take their place in our hearts and command our allegiance. But today you'll have to answer to us all and confess in front of the entire assembly. Today you're going to have to pay."

She turned toward the crowd, the ragged men and women who were watching them, their faces slack with shock. "You might think this doesn't concern you, that it's just between him and the children who were taken away, but it isn't. Do you know what the great Dr. X, savior of Kol, is planning to do next? To raze the Terraces to the ground and relocate you to the Outer Lands! Well, now you know what that means!"

The crowd erupted in angry whispers. A group of young men standing in the front raised their fists and shouted threats to which the guards responded by aiming their guns at them. The men were silenced by their friends, but outraged murmurs continued rippling through the crowd. Anand wondered how long it would take the Terrace dwellers to look around them and realize how powerful they were just by virtue of their numbers. What would they do then?

"Did you expect the city scum to come to your rescue?" Dr. X said to Sumita, his voice as soft and polite as though he was conversing at a dinner party. "You see now how unrealistic your hopes were. In exactly five seconds, I'll give orders to the guards to arrest you and your accomplices. And don't think you can use those hazardous objects against me, because every jammer in the city has been trained on you.

"Oh yes, one more thing. I should express my gratitude

to you in advance because I doubt that you'll be able to register my words by the time the guards are done with you. Thanks to you, as soon as I have the object, I can deal with our friends"—he nodded amicably at the magicians—"who doubtlessly would not have been here without your most eloquent persuasion."

Before Sumita could reply, Commandant Vijay was on his feet. "Don't let him intimidate you! Come over to us, and we'll protect you. We have powers well beyond what you've been led to believe. We'll get you out of here safe, and once we have the mirror in our hands, we'll make sure Dr. X gets punished to your satisfaction."

"The mirror? So! You have two objects of power with you. All the better," Dr. X said. Then he turned to the commandant. "Fool! Didn't you hear me say that all the jammers are turned on full blast?"

"Ah," said Vijay. He clapped his hands once and his companions sprang to their feet. "But we've become more adept at dealing with pain!" He pulled out a long, shimmering peacock feather wand from under his shawl. Similar wands appeared in the hands of his fellow magicians.

"We've been practicing, you see, in our own pain chambers," Vijay continued. "And we're ready for you. Together, we can overpower the guards who are onstage. Long before you can get reinforcements, you'll be dead."

"So will the prisoners," Dr. X said. "Their guards have orders to kill them immediately if there's any violence."

Vijay faltered for a moment, and next to him Basant's mother drew in her breath sharply. But then he said, "We don't care. If you remain in power, you'll kill them anyway. At least this way we'll do maximum damage before we die."

"See what you've done with your silly meddling?" Dr. X said to Sumita, his voice changing to that of a loving, reproachful parent. "There will probably be a huge massacre now—far worse than anything I ever contemplated—and you'll be the cause. Do you want that on your conscience? If not, you had better hand that pack to me."

Sumita looked around at the thousands of people who had come to the Maidan because of her entreaties. Anand could tell that Dr. X had shaken her. The resolute set of her lips wavered, and an uncertainty came into her face. She took a small, swaying step toward Dr. X, who held out his hand as though to a prodigal daughter.

Behind her, Vijay made a hissing noise and raised his peacock feather wand. So did his companions. The guards onstage lifted their guns. A scuffling had broken out near the bullet cars. The prisoners must have rebelled, and the guards were trying to control them. The crowd growled like a dog straining at its leash, ready to join the fray. In a moment the entire assembly would be plunged into a fierce and bloody battle.

There was no time to think. There was no time to speak. Anand did the only thing possible. Pulling out the conch, he blew into it as hard as he could.

THE VISION

There was silence all around Anand. Complete silence and stillness, because every person he looked at—including Sumita and Nisha—was frozen in mid-motion. It was as though he was in a museum, surrounded by wax figures. His heart pounded erratically. He knew how powerful the conch was. Had he, by blowing into it, petrified his friends and all the people of Kol? Had he, in trying to prevent one catastrophe, brought about a worse one?

In the utter quiet, he heard the conch. *There you go again, imagining doom and gloom. Go up to Nisha and shake her gently, and do the same with Sumita. Then listen carefully to what I tell you.*

Anand reached past the frozen snarl of a guard and shook Nisha's arm. She blinked dazedly, and then slid out of the circle the guards had formed around her. Sumita, too, awoke and listened carefully as Anand relayed the conch's instructions.

"Are you sure?" Sumita asked, hugging the mirror protectively. When Anand nodded, she laid the mirror down in the center of the platform. Nisha fetched Dr. X, blank-faced as a sleepwalker, and made him kneel beside the mirror. Anand did the same with the commandant. When the two leaders were positioned face-to-face over the mirror, he clapped his hands thrice. The men awoke with a start, and so did the rest of the crowd. But no one could move or talk as yet.

Anand looked into the glaring faces of Dr. X and Vijay.

"You wanted to see the objects of power," he said. "Well, this is your chance. Look into the mirror."

Dr. X's eyes bulged as he strained to yell a curse at Anand. Vijay, red-faced with fury, made muffled sounds, trying to break free of the spell. At another time, Anand would have been afraid of their rage, but now he merely gripped the conch, drawing comfort from it.

"You don't have a choice," he told them, not unsympathetically. "You were about to destroy Kol, so the objects of power took over. You must do what they want. But don't worry, their power—unlike yours—is benevolent. Now, look into the mirror."

Slowly, reluctantly, the two men bowed their heads. As their eyes met in the mirror, the Pods in the Maidan turned themselves on and gigantic holograms began to form against the brown air. Every face in the crowd stared at them, rapt.

"In exactly five seconds, I'll give orders to the guards to arrest you," boomed Dr. X's hologram, his eyes narrowed to vicious slits. "And don't think you can use those hazardous objects against me, because every jammer in the city is trained on you."

"Come over to us!" Vijay's hologram commanded. "Once we have the mirror, we'll make sure Dr. X gets punished to your satisfaction."

The holograms blurred. Then a new hologram of Dr. X said, with a winning smile, "Hand it over to me peacefully, and I'll promote you to second in command."

It disappeared, and a hologram of Vijay looked around suspiciously. "Almost noon!" it said. "Where are those vermin? Where are the prisoners? This is a trap."

The objects of power were taking the two leaders into the past, one vignette at a time, tracing the course the scientists and magicians had taken to bring their world to this disastrous pass. And it was sharing these with all the inhabitants of Kol so there would be no more lies.

"What do you think will happen after we've seen all of them?" Nisha whispered in Anand's ear.

"I don't know," Anand whispered back. "The magical objects create situations and opportunities, but ultimately humans must make their own choices." He wanted to add that no matter what happened, he would be able to face it because Nisha was with him. But he felt tongue-tied. Perhaps Nisha sensed his feelings, though, for she moved closer, leaning a little against his shoulder. They watched as time rolled backward in a fascinating panorama, revealing answers to the questions that had nagged at them ever since they had arrived in Shadowland.

Of the numerous scenes that flashed past his eyes, later Anand would most remember these:

In the lab, the X-Finder begins to drone, a sound that grows increasingly high-pitched until Sumita and her assistants are forced to clip shields over their ears.

"Look," she says excitedly, speaking into a magnifier so they can hear above the machine's deafening whine. She points to a screen with flashing red dots. "The Finder's search rays have broken the barrier and gone into a different world. I didn't think it could do it! It's found something! I think it's powerful! More powerful than we had hoped for. Look at the needle on the energy gauge—it's all the way over to the right! Someone go and fetch Dr. X—"

The hologram wavers. Suddenly it is night—a simulated moonless darkness. The black hulk of the lab looms ahead. A line of men creeps toward the entrance. "When I raise my hand," the leader whispers, "focus your mental powers on the door locks, all at once. It'll hurt terribly because of the jammers, but you can do it! Once we're inside, place the Detonatrixes on as many machines as you can. We'll meet out here as soon as you're done. In case you get caught, I want you to know how proud I am of you!" He puts his hand on the shoulder of one of the boys—for there are children in the group. The boy turns his face, his smile swaying between fear and courage. It is Basant.

Here is a new scene, inside a classroom. Boys and girls in the white bodysuits marked with a logo that identifies them as apprentice scientists are listening to Dr. X lecture. He is younger, with a full head of black hair and a spring to his step. He strides to the wall screen, points to a problem that flashes there, and asks a question. Two girls raise their hands. Dr. X nods at one, who answers. The answer must be an excellent one, for Dr. X walks over to the student and pats her shoulder. There is genuine affection in his gesture. The other students stare jealously. The commended one bows, then turns to flash her classmates a triumphant grin. Anand sees that it is Sumita, younger, prettier, with a mop of curly hair framing her face. Her forehead is innocent of frown lines. When she looks at Dr. X, her eyes shine with adoration.

Anand can't help glancing from the hologram to the real Sumita standing on the platform. Her face is very pale, and she surreptitiously brushes teardrops from her lashes. He understands that a part of her still loves Dr. X, who was the closest she had had to a father.

Now they are in front of a row of shabby buildings, and with a start Anand recognizes them as the Terraces. A group of children are saying good-bye to their families. A large hover bus, impressively new, waits nearby. The families appear both proud and worried.

"Be sure to write every week, Asha," a woman tells a pig-tailed girl, who nods vigorously.

"Sir," a quavery-voiced old woman—Sumita's grand-mother, perhaps—asks a scientist who is waiting beside the van with barely disguised impatience. "You promise you'll bring them back soon to visit?"

"Of course!" says the scientist, flashing his teeth in a smile. "They can come and see you whenever they want."

Now the projections change color, turning pale sepia. Anand guesses that the scenes being projected now are older, that they occurred before what Dr. X and Vijay can consciously remember. He sees a half-built structure, its shiny, reflective walls identifying it as Futuredome. Around it there is a jumble of men with digging machines. Dust rises from gashes in the earth, or perhaps the air is turning brown? There are no trees. Have they died already? Guards shout at the laborers to work harder. They point their tubeguns at laggards, who drop to the ground in pain. He sees gates being armed with machines and guards. He sees towers where jammers are being strategically positioned to cover all of Kol.

In the next scene, families are leaving their homes at night, their movements hushed and hurried, taking only what they can fit into cars they have enchanted to look old. It is the exodus of the magicians. They travel to a poor part of Kol, with garbage heaped on the streets and buildings with cracked-glass windows. They hide their vehicles in junkyards and enter houses that are little more than hovels. There they sit in a circle, holding hands, weaving a spell that will keep them and their few magical objects from being found by the scientists. Outside, sirens scream; bullet cars cross and recross the skyways, searching. In the morning, their stately, deserted homes are taken over by the Security Council, and the best dwellings and belongings are awarded to the council's new favorites. In a hovel, a boy of perhaps five years sits on the floor, chewing on hard, day-old bread. Could it be Vijay? He turns his face in the direction of the home he has lost, his face twisted with hate.

An even older scene takes shape above their heads, a council chamber where scientists huddle together. No one in this scene wears masks yet. Someone says, "We must call the magicians back to the council and apologize. Without their cleansing spells, the air's turning brown."

But the others refuse. One says, "We're better off without them. They're always objecting to whatever we suggest, holding us back."

"Remember how upset they were when we suggested genetic experimentation so our livestock would eat less and produce more milk?" another adds. "They wouldn't even agree to treat fruits with growth enhancer. They'll never approve our plans for Futuredome or the Farm."

"Maybe they're the ones poisoning our air," someone else says, coughing.

"Their magical objects are what make them so powerful and so arrogant. Maybe they need to be relieved of a few of them," a fourth scientist declares.

Now the scene changes to an earlier council meeting

where different groups are still present: scientists in white uniforms, magicians in elaborate cloaks and shawls. People are arguing vociferously. The leader of the magicians, a gray-haired woman, demands that the council passes a law requiring a more stringent lifestyle for all—especially the scientists, who have grown overly fond of luxury. Several scientists bristle at this comment. Ignoring them, she points out the growing problems around them—prolonged droughts, receding oceans, dying animals, withering crops, air that is increasingly harder to breathe.

"That's why we need more experiments, so we can increase crop productivity," a scientist says. "But your people are always vetoing our ideas."

"Tampering with nature is dangerous—you've seen that already," another magician says, rising to his feet. He reads out the most recent crime statistics. "Robbery and vandalism have increased to such an extent that the police force can no longer handle it," he ends.

"That's why we've recommended the creation of a larger elite police force," says a scientist. "We've allotted enough money in our budget to buy them the best cars and firearms. And we've come up with a highly advanced weapon that doesn't require bullets—"

"I'm against that," a magician says emphatically. "Violence against our own people is no solution. If we want to reduce crime, we have to fill their empty stomachs."

"That's exactly what we are trying to do with our new

methods," a scientist says. "What are *you* doing, except for accusing us?"

"Everything became worse after you performed those weather modification experiments, sending rockets filled with chemicals into the sky," a magician shouts. "You said it would bring rain, but it made the drought worse."

"The experiments might have worked if you had cooperated with us and used your mind power to boost the rockets higher into the stratosphere," yells a scientist. "You probably sabotaged us, just so you could prove that we were wrong."

"Not that you had a better solution," says another scientist. "All you want is to keep us stuck to the old ways, doing rain chants—"

"I refuse to listen to such insults," cries a magician, jumping up. "You have no understanding of how hard we work to keep the energies of the earth balanced, to heal things. We just can't heal them as fast as you're destroying them—you and your cohorts, the machine manufacturers who refuse to follow the safety guidelines we set."

"Ladies and gentlemen!" cries the leader of the scientists, an old man who takes off his spectacles and rubs tiredly at his eyes. "Order, please! We must work together to find a solution to this situation." But no one pays any attention. They yell at each other until the magicians walk out in a huff.

And now the hologram grows very faint, almost transparent, as though the scene above them is being resurrected from a truly distant past. Anand sees the inside of a laboratory, though this is a very different room with its wide-open windows from which trees can be seen. People sit at long tables. They are all dressed in white coats, so Anand cannot tell which group they belong to. They are working on projects together. Someone—perhaps a scientist?—types something into a computer. Someone else waves his hands and chants, and the image on the screen changes. In a corner, two women pore over a liquid bubbling in a beaker, discussing what diseases it might heal. Elsewhere, a magician enunciates a spell and conjures up the model of a city. Her partner admires the structure and points out how the foundations of the tallest skyscrapers can be strengthened.

A bell rings, signaling the end of the work week. A man with glasses—is he the leader Anand noticed in the earlier hologram?—suggests that they all go out for dinner. Among laughter and quips, the men and women stream out into the multicolored evening. They sit at a crowded street-side café, under a Krishna Chura tree laden with flame-colored blossoms, passing bowls of food to each other. Passersby, smiling to hear their infectious laughter, do not know who is a scientist and who is a magician, and they do not care.

It was evening by the time the last hologram had faded away, though in the smoky gloom all distinctions of hour or day had long become meaningless. The people stirred, rubbing their eyes as though emerging from an amazing dream. As he looked around, Anand's heart lurched with anxiety. He could tell that the conch had relinquished its control over the crowd. What would the scientists and magicians decide to do now?

"Akshay," he heard a shaky voice call. It was Chief Deepak, Basant's grandfather, rising to his feet. Was Anand imagining it, or did he seem stronger? Basant's mother hurried to offer him her arm, but he strode forward without assistance until he stood in front of Dr. X. "Akshay!" he called again, his voice firmer now. "It is time we called each other once again by our true names, which we had hidden out of fear, or discarded because of our fascination for a different lifestyle."

Akshay. That was Dr. X's true name!

Dr. X stared at him, still dazed.

"Akshay," Deepak said. "You were one of us once—the most talented apprentice I'd ever seen. I don't blame you for forsaking magic. Yours was a restless spirit, and the quick results that science produces called to it. But for the sake of the Powers that you once venerated, I ask you to listen with your heart to what I say now."

Anand stared, astounded. Dr. X a magician? But of course! That was how he had known to use Colorpower when designing buildings in Futuredome. That was why he could use Persuasion so consummately. That was why he had been able to forestall the magicians whenever they attempted to destroy his machines.

The chief continued, "Both our people have made mistakes. We've hurt each other in many ways. But today we were reminded that once we were friends. Once we helped each other create a better world. Can't we put our wrongs behind us and try to live that way again?"

The old chief extended a trembling hand to Dr. X and another to the commandant. "Come, Vijay," he called. "Let us join hands in amity."

Vijay did not look too happy, but after a moment he came forward and held the chief's hand. The other magicians followed him, promising the old man their cooperation. Anand held his breath, watching Dr. X. What he did now would make all the difference. Vijay, too, was watching Dr. X intently, his eyebrows knotted. Anand knew that he would not tolerate any disrespect to his uncle. Dr. X hardened his jaw and raised his chin. He was going to disagree—Anand was sure of it. The air rippled with tension. The guards raised their tubeguns.

No, no! Anand cried silently, fisting his hands so tight that the nails cut into his palms. *To come so far and lose like this!*

He sensed a movement out of the corner of his eye. Swiveling, he saw Sumita. She crossed the stage and, without taking her eyes from Dr. X, gripped Chief Deepak's outstretched hand. Asha came and stood by her side, then another scientist, and another, until Dr. X was left alone.

Dr. X's shoulders slumped for a moment. Then he took a deep breath and shrugged. "You've won," he said with a strange smile, and put out his hand to clasp the chief's fingers.

TROUBLE

Anand walked up and down Sumita's living room, waiting for the scientist to return. Every few minutes he glanced at the timekeeper on the wall and sighed. Nisha, who was watching a comedy program on the Pod with grim determination, rolled her eyes at his impatience. But he knew she was just as anxious. It was their seventh afternoon in Shadowland. Unless they returned to the Silver Valley in the next few hours, their quest would fail.

Neither of them had eaten anything all day, though Sumita had urged them to help themselves to whatever was in the freeze cube.

"You can eat the leftover chicken curry for lunch. If the council meeting goes on too late, go ahead and have the vacuum pacs of rice and lentil soup for dinner. There are mega-bananas on the table—enjoy them while you can. From next week on, everything's going to be rationed." She had waved them good-bye as she rushed to the elevator.

That was yesterday. Why hadn't she returned, and why hadn't she called?

From time to time, Anand peered out of the window, hoping to spot Sumita's hover van, though he doubted that he'd be able to spot anything at all through the haze outside. Yes, even inside Futuredome the air was brown. The first decision the New-Kol Council had made—though not without some fiercely heated debates—was to start dismantling the domes. The power thus freed up was currently being stored in the lab. Soon they would start using it to improve conditions in the more beleaguered parts of the city.

"The scientists were the loudest opponents, of course!" Sumita had told them after that meeting, which had taken place immediately following the summit in the Maidan. She had come home late that night with her hair frazzled but her eyes bright with plans. "At first, Dr. X was the most vociferous. You can't blame him. It's hard to give up your place at the top of the pyramid. For a while I was afraid he'd win. He can be very convincing when he tries. But the council, which is now made up of magicians and guards and Terrace dwellers as well as scientists, managed to push the reforms through. So, all the domes except for the Farm have had their Fresha-Vents and Simulo-Suns turned off. We'll have to wear masks until things start getting better. And even with everyone cooperating, that'll take quite a while. It's a pain, but I don't mind. So many exciting things are happening! The jammers have been deactivated, and with them gone, the magicians are slowly regaining their powers! Already, Commandant Vijay gave us lessons in a breathing technique that allows you to cleanse the air as you're inhaling it. They're quite amazing, the magicians. And all this time I thought they were Kol's worst enemies!"

Early yesterday Anand and Nisha had been asked to meet with the council in the conference room on the top floor of the lab. A shiver had traveled down Anand's spine as he remembered his last trip to this building, but this time they were honored invitees. They sat at the sleek circular steel table with the council members and drank fizzy Orangeroos in tall narrow bottles—a great honor, Sumita had said, for Futuredome's stock of Orangeroo was fast dwindling. Pretty soon, everyone would be drinking only water, sipped through purifier straws. They were thanked formally for their part in what everyone was calling the Reconciliation. For the most part, it seemed to be working. A few magicians and scientists still shot each other suspicious looks, and Dr. X maintained an icy silence in the background, but for the most part people were eager to be friends. Anand and Nisha were particularly interested to see that Vijay sat next to Sumita, dressed in a brand-new royal blue bodysuit, his hair neatly combed. A couple of times, they caught him smiling at something she said. When it was time to leave, he held the door open for her with a flourish, and Anand could have sworn he saw Sumita blush.

Once the niceties had been observed, the councilors

brought up the real reason for the invitation: the magical objects. Knowing that they longed to feel their power, Anand took out the conch and held it up. As he had hoped, the conch sent forth its calm, golden warmth into the room. Then Nisha took the mirror around the table, allowing each person to look into it. Some drew in their breaths sharply at what they saw, while others gazed silently. Chief Deepak said, "We're eager to learn what the mirror and conch can do to help us with the difficult task of reconstruction that lies ahead."

Anand closed his eyes to commune with the objects of power. "The mirror is willing to stay with you until it is needed elsewhere," he said. "It will remind you of magical arts you've forgotten, or scientific techniques you've lost. The conch must return home with Nisha and me tomorrow in order to restore our ruined valley to its original condition, but before it goes, it promises to help you. Choose a project—whichever one you consider most important—and it will make sure you succeed.

The councilors were disappointed to realize that they would lose the conch, but soon they were engaged in an animated argument as to which project they should choose. Finally, they decided that they wanted to send up another rocket to seed clouds.

Asha said, "This time we'll be careful and use only safe chemicals, the ones everyone agreed upon—and hopefully, it'll result in rain."

"If rain comes," Vijay added, "it'll remove some of the impurities in the air. Then our cleansing spells will work faster."

Sumita said, "If there's enough rain, perhaps even the river—which is all sludge and garbage now—will start to flow."

Dr. X, who had not participated in the discussion so far, suddenly turned to Anand and Nisha. "It'll take a while to set up the rockets. Why don't you rest in S—uh—Sumita's apartment until then. She'll fetch you once we're ready so you can be part of this memorable event." They sprang up, thankful to leave, but as they turned to go, he spoke again. His voice dipped, seductive with Persuasion, but used with great subtlety so that no one else in the room noticed it—no one except Deepak, who looked up with a slight frown. "Leave the objects of power with us. Their presence will inspire us to set everything up more quickly—and that will ensure that you get home on time."

The unexpected request, along with the unethical use of the skill—for it was forbidden to use Persuasion among friends—shocked Anand. While he didn't mind leaving the mirror with the council—it was, after all, going to remain with them—he was uneasy about parting from the conch. But there was no way he could refuse Dr. X without forcing a confrontation, especially as the other councilors, touched by X's Persuasion, added their requests to his.

He handed the conch to Sumita. Sensing his reluctance,

she squeezed his shoulder reassuringly. "Don't worry! We'll be very careful with it."

But he did worry. He tossed and turned in his bed through the night, waiting for Sumita to return. All day he fretted, wondering why she did not send them a Pod-message explaining her delay. Had Dr. X, with his unscrupulous use of Persuasion, brainwashed the council into deciding that the conch was too valuable to give back?

A frantic knocking made Anand and Nisha jump. As they ran to open the door, Anand wondered why Sumita didn't punch in the code on her keypad. But it wasn't Sumita outside. It was Basant, hair askew, panting as though his chest would burst because he didn't have an elevator code and had had to run all the way up the stairs.

"Something terrible has happened," he gasped. "You have to come to the lab right away!"

AN UNEXPECTED TURN

Tearful and grim-faced, Basant's mother drove them to the lab in a car that threatened to die whenever she braked. On the way, Basant told them what he knew, which wasn't much. He had been up all night talking to his mother, telling her about his life in the rehabitational. Toward dawn, he had fallen asleep, only to be jolted awake by an intense pain in his head. Even before he was fully conscious, he recognized it as a blast from a jammer. But how was that possible when all the jammers had been deactivated? Through the jangling pain in his head he heard his uncle Vijay's voice trying to send him a message. It was rushed and incomplete, for Vijay's pain must have been far worse. Basant gathered this much: While the scientists and magicians were hard at work on the roof of the lab setting up the rocket, Dr. X managed to open the vault where the conch and mirror had been placed for safekeeping. He took them and locked himself into the regulator center, which housed the X-Converter and controlled all the security related to the lab as well as the missiles that were positioned along the borders of Kol.

Dr. X locked all entrances into the lab, shut down the Insta-communicators, and announced on the intercom that unless the new council—now trapped on the roof—disbanded in the next two hours, he would activate the missiles, turning them on the most densely populated parts of Kol. However, if the council handed him control of the city, he would give them something far more valuable than what their far-fetched rain project could produce. He would harvest the objects of power in the X-Converter as he had originally planned, thus creating an enormous storehouse of energy that would last the citizens of Kol for years. He ended by warning them that if they tried anything foolish, he would blow up the lab with everyone—including himself—in it.

"Uncle Vijay thinks you two are their only hope," Basant said. "Can you help them?"

Bitter regret filled Anand's mouth. Why hadn't he insisted on staying back at the lab with the conch? Maybe then this catastrophe could have been prevented. "We'll do our best," he said. He closed his eyes and tried to contact the conch, but a giant fist slammed into his skull, driving him to his knees.

"The jammers have certainly been activated," he said through clenched teeth when he could speak. "And they've been notched up, too. I can't reach the conch—and I must, if we're to have the minutest chance of succeeding."

Nisha grasped his hand. "Try again. I'll call some of the

pain into myself. It won't be as bad if it's shared."

Anand hated to cause her any hurt, but the gravity of the situation was greater than his own desires. He nodded.

Basant leaned across the seat and clasped his other hand. "I'll help."

"And I," his mother said, stopping the car to lay a palm on Anand's shoulder.

This time, too, the pain from the jammers surged into Anand, but he could feel it draining out from his body into those of his friends. Their gasps of pain hurt him in a whole different way, though. But their efforts had worked. He was able to catch a small, stuttering pulse of energy. It was the conch.

Come to the front entrance. I'll distract X. Use Transformation to get in. The words grew fainter. *Find the control cen—* The message melted into the pain in his head.

"But where's the control center located?" Anand shouted desperately. But the conch had fallen silent.

"I can take you there," Basant said. "That's where we went on our last mission."

"What will we do after we get there—*if* we manage to get that far?" Nisha asked.

But Anand didn't know the answer to that.

⌇⌇⌇

The three of them stood in front of the massive steel wall that was the entrance to the control center. So far, things had gone smoothly. Sharing the pain with his friends, Anand was able to unlock the main door by using Transformation.

Perhaps the conch had weakened the jammers, for the pain was less debilitating. Once inside, he feared that they would be apprehended by guards on whom Dr. X had used Persuasion, but the corridors were eerily empty. They had reached the control center, but now they were stumped. The door to the center—for there must be one somewhere in the massive wall they were facing—was completely invisible. In spite of focusing his total attention on it, Anand couldn't feel its shape.

"Do you know where the door is?" he whispered to Basant, but the boy shook his head.

"The whole wall looks different," he whispered back. "I think Dr. X has added a magical protection to it."

Though Anand couldn't see or hear Dr. X, he could sense the energy on the other side of the wall. It was at once hot and agitated, like a bull raging around a pen, and cold and lethal, like a cobra waiting to strike.

Conch, he called, *make him open the door.*

The conch's response was still alarmingly feeble. Anand remembered what it had said earlier about the lab draining its power. *I'm sorry, Anand. If I force him to obey me, I would break his mind. I cannot do that. The only thing I can do is to send you energy.*

Anand felt a tingling in his face. The sensation moved down his entire body until he felt weightless. Then it was gone, but he could now hear faint voices from inside. Dr. X was talking to someone.

"No! I've made up my mind. I'd much rather die, taking all of you with me, than have to beg permission from a bunch of nincompoops every time I needed to sneeze. Already, in a couple of days, you've destroyed what I toiled to build over an entire lifetime."

"You're seeing only what you want to see," the other voice said. "You always did. The truth is that everyone on the council is ready to respect you. We would welcome you as an advisor—"

"It's Sumita," Nisha whispered into Anand's ear. "She must be talking to him on the intercom."

She spoke in the softest of tones, but trained as he had been in the magical skills, Dr. X must have had extra-acute hearing. "Who's that outside?" he said. "Answer me at once, or I'll press the detonator." His voice rose wildly as he spoke, and Anand had no doubt that, cornered as he felt he was, Dr. X would make good on his threat.

"It's Anand from the Silver Valley," he said. "I have my friends Nisha and Basant with me. We've come to ask you to reconsider your decision."

"Reconsider, reconsider!" Dr. X gave a bitter laugh. "As though I didn't know that if I gave in to the council's demands, they would immediately put a collar on me and cart me away to a rehabilitational."

"We would never do that!" Sumita's outraged voice crackled over the intercom.

"If you don't, it's only because you're too weak," Dr. X

spat. "You think you can handle this city? Why, it'll be over-run with Terrace vermin in a week—as soon as they figure out that you're too soft to discipline them. Enough talk! Your two hours are up. I'm going to harvest the objects of power, and with that energy I'm going to blow Kol sky-high!"

Anand stood aghast. He wanted to force open the door with Transformation, but he feared that the slightest move might push Dr. X over the edge. Inside the room, he could hear a steel drawer opening and then clanging shut. Dr. X had taken out the conch and the mirror.

Help us! he called to them.

"Dr. Akshay!" The voice bloomed beside him, silvery as the lotuses that once floated on the lake beside the House of Seeing. It was Nisha; she was using Persuasion, her tone soothing as balm on a burn—but at a level far higher than anything he had heard yet. But would it work on Dr. X, who was a Master of the skill himself?

There was silence inside the room.

"Please trust us. We promise we will not harm you. Let us in. You can lock the door behind us again."

"Why should I listen to you?" Dr. X asked. But he sounded less furious, and there was a note of curiosity in his voice.

"Because we will find you a solution. If you aren't satisfied with it, you can go ahead with your plan and blow up the building." Nisha spoke so reasonably, she could have been asking a child to hand over a toy that might injure it. Only her eyes, squeezed shut, and her sickly pallor indicated the agony she was undergoing to create the spell despite the jammers. Anand put an arm around her shoulders and flinched at the pain that tore through him. Basant grasped her other hand and gasped. Even with their help, Anand doubted that she could sustain the spell for long.

He heard a series of whirring clicks, and a small crack opened in the center of the wall.

"Inside!" ordered Dr. X's voice. "Only the two other worlders! Quickly!"

As soon as Anand and Nisha had squeezed through, the door closed behind them. In front of them stood Dr. X, arms crossed. In the pitiless glare of the overhead lights, he looked older than before, with dark circles under his deep-set eyes. To his side, the X-Converter, which resembled a gigantic oven, yawned darkly. On a table next to it were the mirror and the conch. Anand clapped a hand over his mouth. He longed to call out to them, to rush forward and gather them to him, but he knew that a single wrong move would undo what Nisha had worked so hard to achieve.

"Dr. X? *Dr. X?* What's going on?" Sumita's anxious voice called through the intercom.

Without taking his eyes from Anand and his companions, Dr. X reached out and switched it off. "I was crazy to let you in," he said, his voice rising.

Nisha opened her mouth to speak, but no words came out. She had exhausted all her strength fighting the jammers.

Anand could feel the Persuasion spell disintegrating.

"Street scum like you coming up with a solution! What was I thinking of!" Dr. X shook his head disdainfully and, grabbing the conch and mirror, turned to the X-Converter. He ignored Anand's strangled cry. As he bent to slide them into the machine, the mirror caught the overhead lights and flashed.

And just like that, a solution came to Anand.

"You don't want to compromise with the council, and I understand that," he said. "But if you blow up the place, that's not going to get you what you want, either. What if, instead, you could go away somewhere? Somewhere totally different? A world that didn't have the overwhelming problems of Kol? Where no one knew you, so you could start anew? A world where your enormous intelligence would be appreciated?"

"You're lying," Dr. X said. "There's no place like that." But a look of desperate hope flashed on his face.

"There are many worlds out there, beyond even where imagination can take us, and the mirror has access to them all," Anand said. "I won't pretend to know which one is right for you, but I have no doubt that the mirror does. Look into it, and it will show you."

Scowling, Dr. X pulled at his ear, but Anand could see that he was tempted. "Don't move—not even a hand span," he said. "And say your prayers. Because if this doesn't work, in a moment we'll all be bits of exploded flesh." He gave the mirror a wary glance.

Immediately, a light radiated from the mirror. It wasn't a blinding flash but a diffuse glow, like moonlight from behind a lace of clouds. In it Dr. X's face looked younger, yearning. He stared with rapt attention at what the mirror was depicting. Nisha craned her neck, but Anand held her back. Although he, too, was consumed with curiosity, he knew that the vision was private, meant only for Dr. X.

After a long moment, Dr. X turned to Anand and handed him the conch.

"I'll go where the mirror takes me," he said, sounding surprised at his own decision. Then he gave a deep sigh. They could see his clenched shoulders relax.

Nisha came forward, took the mirror gently from his hands, and placed it on the floor. Sure-footed, unhesitant, as though the mirror had explained to him what must be done, Dr. X stepped onto it. This time the mirror pulsed with a light so bright that Anand flinched and covered his eyes. He felt the conch send forth an answering pulse of energy.

When he removed his hands, Dr. X had vanished.

THE RETURN

Anand stepped from the white hover van—now no longer so pristine—onto the cracked pavement. Nisha, Sumita, Basant, and Vijay were with him. They were in the alley where Anand had found himself upon being transported to Kol eight days ago. But how different it looked already! Much of the street garbage had been carted away to the dumps by the newly formed Youth-Kol group headed by Basant and Ishani. Old buildings were being torn down, and a billboard proclaimed that new structures, built from materials salvaged from the domes, would soon take their place. Anand closed his eyes for a moment to picture the new Kol, glittering festively with those shiny, reflective walls, and his heart gave an exuberant leap. But the next moment anxiety constricted his throat. Dr. X had cost them that last, precious day, forcing them to remain in Shadowland beyond the crucial limit of a week. Now they were returning, but perhaps it was already too late to heal the valley.

"We're repairing the sturdier buildings," Vijay said, pointing to a structure ahead of them. Anand and Nisha saw that broken glass had been replaced and lamps gleamed from behind the windows.

"What's that delicious smell?" Nisha asked. Anand sniffed. Even through his mask, the air smelled like lentil and rice stew.

"We've opened a kitchen on the next street, one of several," Sumita explained. "They're nothing fancy—just spots on the roadside with chairs and tables where people can get a simple, inexpensive meal. They've become more popular than we expected!"

"Folks were starving—not just for food but for company, because the previous laws had forbidden them to gather except when ordered to by the council," Vijay said. "Now they sit together for hours, talking, laughing, gathering news—and gossip!"

Sumita laughed. "You should hear what they've been saying about you and Nisha, the warrior magicians from the distant past!"

Then her face grew solemn. "Must you really leave?"

"Stay with us," pleaded Basant. "We could use you on our Youth-Kol team."

"We'd be honored if you stayed," Vijay added.

Anand shook his head with a smile. "We thank you, but our world needs us, and we've been here longer than we should have," he said. *Too long,* cried a small, worried voice within him. But he did not want to burden his new friends with his fears.

After Dr. X had disappeared into the mirror, Anand and Nisha had been faced with a torturous choice. If they left for the valley at once, they would be able to reach it just as the seventh day ended. But they knew that without the conch to help the launch of the rocket, the rain project would fail again.

"We can't do that to Kol," Nisha had said. And though every fiber of Anand's being cried out to return home, he knew she was right.

Joining the council on the roof, they had explained what had occurred. Amazed though they were at Dr. X's disappearance, the council had put aside their questions and conjectures and focused on setting up the rocket. Finally, in the brown, lightless dawn, with the magicians chanting songs of healing and the conch streaming its energies into the launcher, they sent the rocket into the sky. That was only a few hours ago, but Anand thought he could see the first swirls of clouds.

He missed the mirror, which was now set in the center of the council table in the lab. They had been through so much together. But objects of power belonged to no person and no place. They bestowed themselves where they were most needed. Or where they had a connection of the heart, he thought, touching his pocket.

Sumita removed her mask to kiss Nisha on both cheeks. Giving Anand a hug, she said, "I often wondered how it must feel to have a brother or sister. Well, now I know!

My apartment will feel so empty when I return to it."

Anand returned her hug shyly. He was surprised at the affection he felt for Sumita, considering that a few days back they had been bitter antagonists. How mysterious this changing world was!

Sumita unclasped a chain with a small, glittery pendant from around her neck and gave it to Nisha. "I had this made for you. I don't know if you are allowed to take things from one world to another, but if you are, I hope this will remind you of us." Looking closer at the pendant, Anand realized that it was a piece from the wall of Futuredome.

Vijay stepped forward. "Thank you one final time, on behalf of the council," he said, bowing stiffly. "You saved our people." Then he cleared his throat. "As for myself, I owe you an apology for trying to wrest the mirror from you."

Anand knew it was difficult for the proud commandant to admit his fault. "In your place I might have done the same thing," he said.

Now, though, he was impatient to leave. He took out the conch and felt its heat in his cupped palm. Waving good-bye and grasping Nisha's hand, he said to the conch the words he had longed to say ever since he arrived in Kol.

Conch, take us home.

Thought you'd never ask! the conch replied.

There was a swirling around them, like a cloud of cool fire. It lifted them off their feet, rocking them gently. Against his will, Anand felt his eyelids begin to close. Already the scene in front of him was receding, the figures as tiny as dolls. "It's like a magic tale come to life!" Basant shouted, pointing to them.

Just before Anand's eyes shut, he saw Sumita wiping her eyes. Vijay put an arm around her and kissed her forehead, and he knew that they would soon be married.

He felt moisture on his face. "The rains!" he heard Nisha cry. "It was worth it to stay back!" But what had it cost them? he wondered. The last thing he was aware of before he was whisked into the abyss that lay beneath time was Nisha's hand, that dear, familiar clasp, a comfort in the face of what might come.

Anand found himself lying on hard, icy ground, the air around him so cold that his breath made puffs in the air. Shivering, he scrambled to his feet, brushing crusts of snow off his yellow wool tunic—the same one he had worn on his visit to the hermit's cave. He looked around, disoriented, feeling that something important was missing. He was outside the main entrance to the Silver Valley. Ahead of him, gleaming in the morning sun, was the three-pronged peak he had first viewed when he rescued the conch from the sorcerer Surabhanu and brought it back to its rightful home. And here was the flat rock on which he had stood and requested entry into the valley. He stepped onto the rock once again, his heart beating with excitement and fear and love. What would he see when he spoke the password that

Abhaydatta had given him seemingly a lifetime ago? Had the return of the conch from Shadowland healed the valley, or would he enter it to find only a frozen wasteland? If so, what would he and Nisha do?

With that thought he realized why he had been feeling so uneasy. Nisha was missing, and so was the conch. He searched frantically in his pockets but could not locate it. His breath came in gasps and he felt dizzy. Somewhere in the abyss of time—as once before—he had lost them both, his beloved conch and his best friend. But no, she was more to him than that, though his panicked mind couldn't find the right words.

The conch is too powerful to get lost! he reminded himself. *And it'll protect Nisha.* Still, his voice shook as he spoke the password.

He waited for the peaks to split open with a great rumbling sound, for a shining gateway of crystal to appear in the opening, for the healer who guarded the gate to welcome him. But nothing happened.

Had the conch been unable to heal the valley? Cold fingers of guilt squeezed his lungs.

Conch, he cried, *I've failed you and my brothers.*

He received no answer, but the faintest of smells wafted through the frozen landscape. Was he imagining it, or was it the fragrance of silver parijat flowers?

"I have to get inside and find out," he said in a determined voice. He closed his eyes and focused on the place where the gate should have appeared, using everything he knew of Transformation. It was difficult. His body ached from its journey through the abyss, and his mind was still confused. He took a deep breath and visualized the conch, perfect-fitted in the hollow of his hand. A blinding headache mushroomed inside his skull. But in spite of it, very slowly, he felt a shift in the atoms that made up the rocks in front of him.

Opening his eyes he saw that a crack, just enough for a person to slip through, had opened up in the mountain. And in it stood the affronted gatekeeper.

"I've never seen such impudence!" he cried. "First, you don't return at the time Master Abhaydatta specified, so that your password becomes invalid. Next, instead of waiting penitently at the gate, as you would have if you had an iota of intelligence, you try to push your way in, breaking the guardian spells. Now I'll have to call the Master of Protections to come and fix them—as though he didn't have enough to do already! I have a good mind to leave you out in the cold for another sixteen hours, which is how late you are. But instead I'm going to take you to the Chief Healer, and let him decide how you should be punished."

"Wait," Anand said, "did you say *sixteen hours?*"

The gatekeeper looked at him with irritation, but Anand must have seemed particularly perplexed, so he said, in a slightly kinder tone, "Yes. You were supposed to get back from the hermit's cave yesterday by sunset—don't you remember? You threw the entire Brotherhood in a flurry when you hadn't returned by midnight. Master Somdatta was afraid you'd met with some kind of accident. He was ready to send out a search party. Poor Master Abhaydatta spent all night in the Hall of Seeing, trying to find out what had happened to you. Finally he announced that it was just your stubbornness that made you stay up there longer. As you can imagine, he isn't too happy with you, either."

"Where's the conch?"

"In the Crystal Hall, of course. Where else would it be? Did you fall and hit your head on the way down? You're asking such asinine questions."

As Anand dragged his exhausted body through the gap into the valley, he tried to sort things out. The conch had brought him back to the exact time when he had reached the valley and found it devastated. It had restored everything to normal, and done it so perfectly that the Brotherhood had no inkling of what had happened. Around Anand the parijat trees bloomed, as delicately beautiful as ever. The orchards were laden with ripe fruit. Cows mooed contentedly from their pastures, and in the distance a group of apprentices followed their teacher—from his enormous girth Anand guessed him to be Vayudatta—to the tower where they would learn to decipher messages from the winds, as Anand had once done.

Anand's heart expanded with happiness and pride. He had done it! He had fought his way into Shadowland, battled amazing odds, and brought back the stolen conch, the greatest treasure of the valley. He had saved the Brotherhood.

"You're looking pretty cheerful for someone who's about to get his head chewed off," the gatekeeper commented dryly as he knocked on the door to the Chief Healer's hut. "Wait outside. I'll check whether Master Somdatta has the time to see you now."

Anand waited in a whirl of anticipation. How grateful the Chief Healer would be when he realized what Anand had done! Perhaps he would announce it in the assembly. Perhaps he would give Anand a special award for heroism. Anand could see himself standing in the middle of the Crystal Hall with its delicate, fluted pillars. Master Somdatta would give a brief message—he was a man of few words— thanking and praising him. In obedience to the rules of the Brotherhood, he wouldn't mention the details of Anand's mission, but Anand did not mind that. Great doings often had to be kept secret. He visualized Master Abhaydatta, his face bright with pride at his apprentice's accomplishment, fastening a golden medallion around his neck. Anand would bow modestly. The assembly would erupt in applause. And right in the front row would be Nisha, clapping the loudest, her eyes bright with admiration. Later, she would throw her arms around his neck and—

His reverie was interrupted by the gatekeeper. "The healers are in a meeting. Master Somdatta will see you at night. Meanwhile, he sends you this." Almost apologetically, he handed Anand a piece of parchment.

Anand was a trifle disappointed, but he unrolled the parchment with a smile. In a moment the smile faded. On the parchment was written: *In light of his disobedience, the healers have decreed that, starting now, Anand must clean the cow byre for an entire week.*

Anand couldn't believe his eyes. Instead of the praise that was his due, he had been given a punishment—a severe one. Of all the chores in the valley, cleaning out the byre was the most unpleasant. Hot outrage pricked his armpits. Even if they did not know what had really happened, they should have given him a chance to explain. Why hadn't Abhaydatta—his own Master, who should have protected him—spoken up on his behalf, insisting that they hear his side of the story? That hurt more than anything else.

He crumpled up the parchment, shot the gatekeeper a burning look, and stormed down the path. He wished he could talk to Nisha. She would have understood the full weight of the unfairness to which he'd been subjected. She would have sympathized. But she was in the gorge of herbs. The only one with whom he could share his anger was the conch.

A FINAL LESSON

Anand was afraid the Crystal Hall would be full of people who would ask him where he had been for the last four days. He was in no mood to dodge persistent questions—for even in the Silver Valley, people could be very inquisitive. Though he was angry with Abhaydatta, he did not wish to disobey his request that the journey to the hermit's cave be kept secret. Nor did he want, in his agitation, to let slip something about that other, even more secret, journey to Kol.

There were people in the Crystal Hall, as always, but fortunately they were meditating and no one noticed Anand. He strode up to the lotus-shaped shrine where the conch shone, serene in its splendor. A part of his heart flared with joy to see it back in its home, but another part was still angry.

Do you know what your precious Masters have done? he asked the conch silently, though what he really wanted was to shout the words until they ricocheted from the walls.

Sit down and take a deep breath, the conch said. *You look like you're about to have an apoplexy. And that's not going to help the cows.*

You know? You know that they're making me clean out the byre—as though I were a callow first-year apprentice who had run off on a prank? Aren't you going to do anything about this injustice?

And what makes it so unjust? the conch asked innocently.

Anand glared at the conch. *I risked my life to help them. I called up the mirror and crossed the abyss. I rescued you. I helped the people of Kol. I—*

That's a lot of Is, the conch remarked.

Well, Anand conceded ungraciously, *Nisha helped—and so did you and the mirror. But that's not the point.*

What is the point, then? The conch's voice was quiet. But it was a dangerous quiet, and for the first time, Anand hesitated to speak.

You want the Masters to know what you did for them, is that it? the conch asked. *You want me to remind them of how the valley exploded when I was pulled out of it? You want them to suffer again the trauma of being scattered into the abyss—the memory of which I erased from their minds when I brought them back? You want them to be grateful to you—the great Anand—forever, even though it will leave them scarred?* As he spoke, the conch glowed like a ball of iron left in a fire. Even through the crystal walls of the shrine, Anand could feel the scorching heat radiating from it. He heard, for a moment, the shrieking of a terrible wind, followed by the cries of a thousand hapless souls sucked into it. He felt their agony on his skin, in his teeth, deep in the marrow of his bones.

No. His voice came out in a croak as he sank to the ground. His face burned with shame. How arrogant he had been. How selfish in his blindness. *I don't want them to experience that again. I'd rather they never found out. Not even Abhaydatta—especially not him. I don't care if I'm never thanked. I'd much rather clean the byre—for a month, if necessary. And anyway, it wasn't I who restored the valley—I could never have tackled something so huge, I see that now. It was you.*

The heat was replaced by velvet warmth. *We did it together,* the conch said. It spoke no further, but Anand felt forgiven.

After a while, he dared to ask, *The force from the future— was it really stronger than you?*

I've defeated worse things in my time, the conch replied. *Remember Surabhanu? Remember the jinn?*

Then why did you let it pull you from the valley, Anand said in agitation, *when you could have prevented all this pain?*

Sometimes pain is necessary for a greater good, the conch said. *If we hadn't gone into Kol, what would have happened there?*

The people of Kol would have destroyed each other. Or they would have ultimately run out of energy sources and perished. Now they're trying to work together to improve their environment—

Exactly. You, too, learned some things in the course of your journey, though you might not realize their importance yet. And we, the Company of the Conch, had a great adventure. Wasn't that what you had wanted on that day when Abhaydatta called you to the Hall of Seeing? Now you'd better get yourself to the byre before the Animal Master comes looking for you.

As Anand hurried to the byre, something nagged at him. The conch had said, *We, the Company of the Conch, had a great adventure.* The company—that was the four of them: Nisha, the conch, himself, and Abhaydatta. But how could it be an adventure for Abhaydatta—and perhaps Nisha, too—if they didn't remember any of it?

∞

At the byre, empty because the cattle were out grazing, a resigned Anand armed himself with a bucket of water, a shovel, and a scrubbing brush and entered the first stall. He grabbed the shovel in a determined grip, hitched up his robes, and started shoveling manure. But before he had finished even one stall, he heard someone calling his name.

Wiping sweat from his forehead, he stepped outside to find Raj-bhanu, the junior healer who had brought him the message from Abhaydatta—was it only a few days ago? Anand stared at him. Had Raj-bhanu been pulled into Shadowland? Was he the young truck driver who had helped Anand and Nisha escape from Vijay? Anand would never know.

Raj-bhanu greeted him affably, just as he would on any other day. A little distance behind him was a boy of about ten years whom Anand had not seen before. He was thin and buck-toothed and hung back shyly, his stiff new robes

He seemed so distressed that sympathy welled up in Anand's chest. Somehow the boy must have become separated from his own people. A trauma like that could make anyone lose his memory.

"It doesn't matter," he said, putting an arm around the younger boy. "Don't worry. You're safe now. We'll take good care of you, and when you get formally accepted into the Brotherhood, the Masters will give you a new name that will fit you even better than your old one."

Entering the noisy dining hall, Anand looked around for Nisha. His heart beat unaccountably fast as he saw her sitting at a table across the hall, her hair helter-skelter around her face, her shawl awry as usual. She waved at him to join her. He gestured for her to save an additional space, pointing to the nameless boy. When they joined her, she stared at the boy with a small frown. Anand wondered why. But what he most wanted to know was whether Nisha remembered their journey to Kol. How could he ask, though, when they were surrounded by so many people, including this boy with his deep-set, solemn eyes that observed everything?

"There's so much I have to tell you!" Nisha was saying. "The gorge of herbs is absolutely beautiful. I was longing to stay another night, but I knew Mother Amita would have a fit if I didn't return on time. I loved all the birds there, but the parrots were most friendly. I'd taken some nuts, and they sat on my shoulder and ate them from my hand. A large green-breasted one even followed me halfway up! But how was your journey? And who's the boy with you?"

It took Anand all his willpower to answer Nisha's questions and introduce the new boy. She had forgotten! The conch had taken the memory of Kol from her. He didn't doubt the wisdom of the conch's act, but his chest felt hollow and dark. Now he had no one with whom to discuss his adventures in Shadowland. Worst of all, he would never be able to tell Nisha how much her smile had helped him in the midst of the many dangers he had had to face. Loneliness spread through him like fog.

The boy was looking around the hall with great interest. Nisha took this opportunity to whisper to Anand, "There's something about him. Does he look familiar to you?"

Anand stole a look, but he could not tell. His heart was still heavy. To distract himself, he asked the boy, "Do you like the food?"

The boy nodded. "I've never eaten anything like it!"

Anand smiled. He remembered when he'd first come to the valley, a poor boy from the slums of Kolkata, and felt the same way.

The boy raised his glass of milk and drained it in a single gulp. Something about the gesture tugged at Anand's mind, but before he could figure out what it was, a bell rang.

"The Masters—the ones sitting on the dais—are about to make an announcement," he whispered to the boy.

The hall was silent now, every face turned expectantly

toward the Chief Healer, who had risen to his feet.

"We have something to celebrate," Somdatta said. He spoke with his usual softness, but his words penetrated the farthest corners of the hall. "Thanks to two of our own who shall remain unnamed, we have been saved from a great disaster. We will not speak further of this dark event, for it is best not to give such things power through attention. But this much we can say: In honor of the brave young people, the Masters themselves have prepared the desserts today."

Excited chatter erupted through the room as the Chief Healer sat down; everyone was trying to guess the identity of the heroes. Anand felt his cheeks burn. The Masters knew. Somehow the conch had found a way to inform them without making them suffer. He glanced at Nisha, hoping Somdatta's speech had jogged her memory, but she was explaining to the newcomer that the Masters, who rarely cooked, made the best sweets. "Wait till you taste them," she concluded. "I'll bet you really haven't eaten anything like that! I've only had the good luck to try them once, and my tongue still dreams about it."

The Masters were coming through the hall, distributing the sweets themselves. Anand waited in pleasant anticipation. He was even more pleased when he noticed that Abhaydatta, with whom he had longed to speak since his return, was approaching their table, holding a huge tray aloft. Anand and Nisha bowed to him, and the new boy, watching them, scrambled to his feet and bobbed his head in awkward imitation.

Abhaydatta courteously returned the gesture.

To Nisha he said, "I'm glad you've returned safely from the gorge. Please ask Mother Amita if I may have some of the fresh brahmi root you collected there."

To the newcomer he said, "I hope you have made friends with your new guide. Master Somdatta is ready to assign you to a sleeping hall, so be sure to speak with him after you finish eating."

Drawing Anand aside, he said, "The hermit has sent a message. You must have impressed him, for he has agreed to instruct you in the lore of objects of power! You are to go up to his cave once a week, starting tomorrow morning." His eyes twinkled at Anand's gasp of delight. "Indeed, you should be pleased! You're the first student he has accepted in a decade. Come to the Hall of Seeing, and we'll discuss this further. But first, it's time for dessert. I hope you enjoy it. It's a recipe I acquired recently."

He handed them each a small packet wrapped in banana leaf and moved on.

Anand opened his packet and gasped again. How many surprises had this day kept hidden in its folds? A small golden square lay in his hand. It looked exactly like the one the cook had given him at the scientists' party in Future-dome. He took a bite. Beyond a doubt, the taste was the same. He had saved a piece for Nisha, slipping it secretly to her in Sumita's car. How many dangers they had faced that day—and in the days to come! But even in the worst of times, they had drawn strength from each other.

All those memories, lost to her.

He kept his eyes on her, willing her to remember, though he knew it was no use. She popped the sweet into her mouth. A blissful look came over her face as she chewed. Then, just as Anand was about to turn away, she slipped a finger beneath the edge of her shawl. Turning so that only he could see, she pulled out a silver chain and held up the quaint, jagged pendant hanging from it. Then she hid it again.

She hadn't forgotten.

Anand itched with impatience to be alone with her. How much they had to share!

Oh, Conch! he thought, grateful and humbled all at once. *I should never have believed that you'd take something so important away from her—and me.*

The conch's tone was deeply injured. *So many years we've known each other, and that's all the trust you had in me?*

I'm sorry, Anand said, abashed.

But the conch was chuckling. *Fooled you again! It takes a lot more than that to upset a conch—unlike you overly sensitive humans.*

Nisha asked the newcomer, "Doesn't the sweet taste wonderful—and different from anything you've ever had?"

"It's delicious," the boy said. "But I *have* tasted it before—only I can't remember where." He pulled at his earlobe with an abstracted frown, trying to place the dessert. But in a while, he gave up. "Maybe it'll come to me later," he said. "I had better go and talk to Master Somdatta now." He raised his second glass of milk and said, appreciatively, "This milk, too, is excellent, so sweet and creamy."

And suddenly, as he watched the boy drain his glass and excuse himself from the table, things fell into place for Anand. He glanced at Nisha and saw her face mirroring his shock. The boy was Dr. X! The mirror had sent him back to the valley, and somewhere during that journey, the conch had changed him to a child and erased his memory.

Anand shook his head to clear it. How intricately they were woven, the threads that made up this mysterious universe. Now he had even more to discuss with Nisha.

Conch, he asked, *why?*

The conch gave a sigh of mock exasperation. *As I've told you before, on numerous occasions, you must wait and discover these things by yourself. How else will you—*

Grow, Anand supplied with a smile. *Oh, very well. Nisha and I will figure it out.*

You do that, said the conch. *She's blossomed into a fine young lady, our Miss Impatience. She'll keep you on the right track.*

The bell rang, signifying the end of the meal. The apprentices hurried to their lessons and duties. Anand waved good-bye to the newcomer and stepped outside with Nisha. They walked down the path that led to the Hall of Seeing.

The Garden Master and his helpers must have worked here recently, for it was lined with new flowers: Queen of the Night, jasmine, and marigolds. He had so much to say to Nisha, he didn't know where to begin. But strangely, the restiveness that had been gnawing at him through the meal had subsided. Joy spread through him as they made their way along the winding path side by side, in this magical place they both cherished, listening to the *kokils* calling to their mates in the tamarind trees. Anand took a deep breath, relishing the sweet air that he had always taken for granted. How blue the sky was, unfurling over their heads like a blessing. He plucked a marigold colored like the sun and handed it to Nisha, who tucked it behind her ear with a shy smile. Many adventures awaited him—in this valley with Abhaydatta and Nisha, up on the mountain with the hermit, and perhaps in some other new world with the conch. But for now he was content to clasp Nisha's hand, the way she had taken his through so many dark moments.

"It's good to be home," he said.